Becoming Delilah

SARA MARCHANT

Fairlight Books

First published by Fairlight Books 2023

Fairlight Books
Summertown Pavilion, 18–24 Middle Way, Oxford, OX2 7LG

A CIP catalogue record for this book is available from the
British Library

1 2 3 4 5 6 7 8 9 10

ISBN 978-1-914148-26-2

www.fairlightbooks.com

Printed and bound in Great Britain

Designed by Emma Rogers

This is a work of fiction. Names, characters, businesses, events
and incidents are the products of the author's imagination. Any
resemblance to actual persons, living or dead, or actual events is
purely coincidental.

For Kathleen Marie

A Dusty Desert Town
in the West

Her name, Dolores, was embroidered with fancy script on a stocking hanging on the brick fireplace. A tiny golden nail, hammered neatly into the mortar, held it in place. Dolores wanted to hold the soft velvet stocking, heavy with treasure and candy, wrapped gifts and fruit. She wanted to stroke the stiff golden threads spelling out the name she was learning to print in school, the thick pencil clenched in her hand. She knew the stocking would smell of chocolate and pine like the beautiful tree in the corner far from the fireplace; way down in the toe of the sock would be a fat tangerine giving a spicy tang to the *mezcla* of scents. She wanted to upturn the stocking into her mother's lap, the silky-soft skirt between Mama's knees pooling into a perfect bowl, wanted to dump out her prize and put her face into the opening of the fur-lined sock. Maybe her whole head would fit inside it, like with Santa's furry hat. She wanted to inhale the dark, soft safety inside of it.

The stocking was new and beautiful, the embroidery Abuela's work: Dolores recognized it as surely as the scent of talcum or the Tabu lipstick her grandmother applied every morning. These scents gave Dolores comfort, a feeling of safety. She was named for her beautiful, sweet-scented maternal grandmother, whom everyone called 'Abuela', even Daddy, so it felt like another gift when Dolores learned they shared a name. Mama had told her right before Daddy spied the little gold nail.

Dolores was five, but she recognized danger in Daddy's glare at the tiny nail holding up her bulging stocking. He hadn't placed the nail there in the mortar; no one had asked his permission to mar the perfection of the red-smelling brick or the musty cement of the newly cleaned grout. Mama had scrubbed for days, Dolores trying to help but mostly getting in the way – she knew because Mama sometimes wept while preparing for the holiday – but now they had broken another of his unwritten rules. These rules, Daddy's special rules, were never usually known until after they had already been broken. Dolores was five, but her whole life had been lived under the threat of rules, known or not, being broken. In that moment, the scent of the tree in the corner and the smoky fire, and the turkey roasting in the nearby kitchen, was overpowered by the sharp, metallic odor of Mama's fear. Dolores tried to embrace her, but Mama pushed her away, shoving her further from danger, from Daddy. Dolores was behind Mama, then was pulled further back by Abuela.

No one dared to take the stocking down and give it to Dolores while Daddy had that look or held his shoulders so tense, his hands curled into fists. When he finally stood from his black vinyl recliner and stepped towards Dolores's stocking, she wasn't glad that she'd be allowed to open whatever small, individually wrapped gifts were inside, eat the tangerine from the toe or share the sweet chocolates laced throughout. Daddy stroked the tiny nail pushed into the mortar, breathed heavily once out of his nose, and Dolores knew to hide behind her grandmother's small body for protection. Even Daddy wouldn't dare hit Abuela.

'Take her, Mama,' Dolores's mama said. Even now she spoke English, because speaking Spanish was against Daddy's rules. Dolores was never to be taught Spanish. Mama didn't look away from Daddy as she spoke to her own mama. 'Take her and go.'

Dolores looked over her shoulder at her mother as Abuela pulled her from the room, out of the house, towards safety. Her mother was so small, standing there in her Christmas finery. Stepping towards Daddy, towards danger. The pale green silk of her dress – Dolores had stroked its cool slipperiness earlier – shivered as Mama tucked loose tendrils of her upswept hair back into the pins, her hands trembling. She looked like the tiny Palo Verde tree that struggled to grow in the backyard when the fierce desert winds blew, its thin pallid needles whipped this way and that but never ripped free. This image of her mother as a tree, a tiny sapling about to be broken by the wind, was the one Dolores lived with for the rest of her life.

It was the last time Dolores set eyes on her. Her mother never looked back.

The Island

Her name was Delilah. Or at least that's what she told the sheriff. The village matriarchs, led by Mrs Oakapple, said it sounded made up. They didn't know her name at first, naturally. It would be weeks before they learned it. Those who knew her in a business or official capacity refused to divulge any information on the girl, precisely because of their official capacity. That's how they all referred to her before they knew her name, and often even afterwards: 'the girl'. (She looked barely out of her teens – too young for them to think of her as a woman.) They were taciturn by nature, and their environment required tact, discretion and independence.

It was an island, you see. It was an East Coast island, not a West Coast or a Mediterranean island. It wasn't the tropical breeze and swaying palm tree kind. It was a tall pine moaning with sea gusts and unexpected hurricanes hurling their way off the Atlantic kind of island. It was not paradisical, although it could be beautiful. The inhabitants worked hard for any beauty. The year-round islanders were therefore a bit sturdier than the average mainlander, tougher, but their village – there was only one on the island – was just lovely.

On this island off Cape Cod there was a small cottage for sale. The cottage shared a driveway with a larger, yellow-painted house where a man lived alone. The driveway was wide and unpaved; its gravel petered out towards the end, where it segued into beach sand

and sharp seagrass right after the cottage's dilapidated garage. The inconvenient shared-driveway arrangement was thought to be the reason the cottage lingered on the market; who wanted to share? The larger saltbox house had a detached garage at the front of the driveway. The cottage's garage, beyond a cramped backyard, a few paces away from where the beach dunes began, was also detached. This would be important later on.

One day in late winter, a taxi left the girl and her baggage at the cottage. She had the keys and went in. She almost immediately walked back out to prop open the door with a deckchair that had seen its best days thirty years before. The islanders were able to track the girl's movements in the house by the windows that she forced open with bangs and exhalations of frustration. The cottage had been a rental for most of its existence, and they all knew in what state renters left a place. Surreptitiously, the village housewives shook their heads in sympathy for the cleaning task the girl faced.

But if the girl *wasn't* enjoying her task, she gave no sign. She spent the first month deep-cleaning the cottage, wearing overalls and no make-up, her black hair tied back with the type of thick white rubber band that came round the delivered newspaper and, once removed, was tossed into a kitchen junk drawer as too useful to be thrown away. When not cleaning, the girl paced the front garden, a pen and notebook in hand. She was making plans. Her neighbors watched and discussed her. The man next door watched, too, but had no one with whom to discuss her. He kept himself to himself.

On the weekends, she maintained her schedule of cleaning, clearing and pacing, but took frequent breaks on the front porch and watched the street. She was waiting. It was more than a month before her waiting was rewarded. It was almost, but not quite, warm enough for her to be wearing a flouncy dress instead of her overalls the afternoon when a little sports car drove up and a city type, too old for his long hair and overly blue denim jeans, unfolded from the vehicle to embrace her. He was tall, so tall that when he picked her up to kiss her red mouth, her skirt hitched up high on her thighs. One of her shoes fell off and the sleeve of her dress slipped down off her shoulder. The watching villagers disapproved of this. The watching man in the neighboring house did not.

What about that girl? the villagers asked each other. Who was she really? How could she afford a beachfront cottage on an island where real estate was hard to come by and increasingly pricey, even for potting sheds? After two months she showed no sign of employment – or contrariwise, any sign of being independently wealthy. There were a few of those on the island: the independently wealthy. They weren't much liked. Everyone, led by Mrs Oakapple, assumed the man in the house sharing a driveway with the girl was one of them.

The girl couldn't be rich, because she didn't own a car. If she wasn't able to walk to an area on the island, she rode an old rust-colored bicycle she'd found in the detached garage. The bike had a decrepit basket wired to the front, which she used for carrying groceries or small plants she bought at the nursery. She was polite to the shopkeepers, she smiled at babies and the aged, she obeyed all traffic laws, but she never engaged in conversation.

'At least she doesn't keep a cat,' said Mrs Oakapple to Mrs Bradshaw as they stood outside the pharmacy, watching the girl pedal away. 'I can't abide a cat.'

Delilah smiled a lot while riding the bike, but not actually *at* anyone; the islanders appreciated the difference. She started a tab at the grocery store and the hardware store like almost every other islander, and this might have endeared her to them, but unlike the islanders the girl didn't settle up weekly or monthly when her paycheck arrived and every other necessity had already been paid. The girl's monthly tab was mailed to an office address on the mainland and a check was promptly returned. This timely remittance did endear the girl and her long-haired benefactor signing the checks to the proprietors of the village shops. But they were very careful not to mention it out loud. It was no one's business how the girl paid her bills, nor how the proprietors appreciated it.

Her dress was another area of status confusion. Most days she wore baggy overalls and shirts, a black swimsuit – so old that white elastic threads waved from it – for beach swimming, and cut-offs with a tank top for her daily morning run. Except when the boyfriend was in town, that is. Then the flouncy dresses appeared or the skirts, lace camisoles and tight cap-sleeved peasant blouses, and bikinis for swimming or walking the shore with the tall man. She had two wardrobes because she had two lifestyles: weekday and weekend.

It did not take much imagination for the watching villagers to mark the situation as sordid. A beautiful young woman – has it been mentioned that the girl was beautiful? Or maybe that was a given? – and a rich older man who provided a secluded house and a comfortable living in exchange for... what, exactly? The monthly or bi-monthly weekend wherein who knew what occurred? No one *knew*, but everyone had their suppositions.

No one ever spoke to the neighbor, so no one knew what his suppositions might be. There was never an opportunity to speak with the man in the yellow house. He avoided society so assiduously that eventually island society avoided him, and they thought it was their own idea. When he drove off in his old car, heads turned in order to not see him.

He went for a daily run, too. Sometimes his run overlapped with Delilah's. They'd pass on the beach – at most a nod was exchanged;

maybe eyes met. If they happened to be running in the same direction, distance was maintained. They certainly never spoke. Surely someone would have seen if they had stopped to speak.

Spring weather concentrated the girl's attention on the front garden. The new soil, now settled, was planted. Surprising the villagers, she planted it as a kitchen garden. The original plantings around the periphery remained, however, showing she had some common sense. Sighs of relief were heaved over the fact that she hadn't ripped out the mature plantings and thrown those away as well. 'She may be no better than she should be,' Mrs Oakapple told Mrs Thompson at the clinic's annual charitable drive, 'but at least she isn't wasteful.'

'She put a kitchen garden in her front yard,' one of the younger, less stoic housewives said to her mother in an aside. Someone capable of such heresy outside was capable of practically anything in private. 'What do you suppose the inside looks like when she's given away all the furniture?' Her mother shushed her – admitting to curiosity was blasphemous as well – but patted her daughter in sympathy; it was human nature to wonder, after all.

The women of the island relaxed in silent relief when the girl in the cottage dragged the bicycle from her garage, packed a picnic in the basket and hopped on. Clean was clean, but obsessively clean made the rest of them look bad. Yes, they were relieved when the girl stopped cleaning and started bicycling around the island to study other gardens. It was harder to keep track of her, but her sudden appearance riding through one's neighborhood kept life interesting. It was almost an honor if she paused to study your garden. She had better manners than to actually speak to anyone. Her exploration of the island led to other, more unsavory situations, but the islanders weren't to know that at first.

The shared driveway was on Mulberry Street, but it didn't look like a driveway. It looked like a graveled lane that led to the beach – which is what it was when Mrs Oakapple was a toddling girl, before all this oceanfront property was built, back when the grass-covered dunes went on for miles. But now, the cottage's garden gate faced the driveway; there was no entrance from the sidewalk that ran parallel to the front fence. It was a white picket fence, of course. In order to reach the cottage's front porch, one was required to enter the driveway, walk about ten feet, turn right into the garden gate and then left onto the three front steps. It could be considered awkward if one had the sort of mind that thought of things like that. It seemed the girl didn't.

The house next door was originally perched on stilts the way island houses off the Carolinas were built, but sometime in its past it was finished so that the stilts disappeared and it was merely a very tall house, the front of which was mostly hidden by the garage at the mouth of the driveway. There was a large blue spruce tree behind the garage, shading what space remained as well as the house's tiny porch, dark and dismal all seasons of the year. It did have a gate on Mulberry Street, but it had been locked and overgrown with displaced seagrass so long ago that even the postman forgot about it and any circulars addressed to the house were left in the box for Delilah's cottage, freshly painted and with its screws tightened by the girl, so it sat jauntily on the picket fence. Not that either address received much mail, nor that the postman would discuss such matters in the first place. Even when cleverly questioned by the younger, fairer matrons when their mothers weren't around to stop or scold them.

The back of the house, facing the grassy dunes that led to the sea, ended in a deck. There was a table with an umbrella and chairs there that, as far as the islanders knew, were only used when the man who lived there sat down to tie his running shoes. Or sat down to take them off. Sometimes, in the evening, he appeared to be drinking wine. This gave the villagers pause: a man drinking wine alone on a weeknight. Seemed foreign. Or maybe it was something city people did? Not that anyone was watching him, they were quick to reassure each other.

He went running, and sometimes took the car out. A worker from the electric company read the meter. Twice, a mainland plumber came. A local handyman was hired for odd jobs. Once a month, a man came from an off-island gas company and refilled the tank that reposed, illegally, under the deck. 'Gas oven,' the women said. Who needed gas that often, unless they were baking and cooking every day? The men didn't notice, unless it was to unconsciously sniff at the delicious odors wafting from the open windows – 'At all hours of the day and night, too,' Mrs Oakapple whispered to the postman. Aside from the lights and the scents and the little car leaving the garage, it could be an abandoned house. Perhaps haunted. That brightly painted yellow house could be hiding anything.

At the end of the graveled driveway was a path that meandered among the dunes and the scrubby willow trees that managed to grow where little else besides tough seagrass could. This path ended at the beach proper. The cottage's garage marked the end of the right-hand side of the drive. The left-hand side was about head-level with the flooring of the yellow house's deck. Head-level for Alan, that is, Delilah's tall city man, who parked his car in the garage during his sporadic weekend visits. It was not head-level for Delilah.

At the other end of the driveway, at the entrance to Mulberry Street, two sturdy yet elegantly slim concrete posts stood embedded on either side of the gravel. Iron rings jutted out at the top of each. Delilah never saw the posts, just overlooked them really, until spring began to segue into early, hopeful summer and a few more tourists trickled onto the island, exiting the ferry.

That afternoon she wheeled her bike from the garage, a new nursery catalogue in the basket next to her packed lunch. She walked to the end of the driveway, and stopped. A length of chain was clipped to each post to hang down, barring entrance to the driveway. A small metal sign hung from the middle of the chain. The side facing Delilah was blank. She carefully unclipped the chain from the post on her side of the driveway, pushed the bike through, clipped the chain closed again and then turned to read the sign. *PRIVATE PROPERTY.* She rode away frowning.

Delilah felt the villagers' eyes on her, of course. She'd felt eyes on her before and grown to evaluate what each gaze meant, the motivations behind it, each viewer's intent. But this gaze – the islanders' gaze – felt different. She spent time every day, while she went about her homemaking, garden-planning and now bicycle-riding, parsing why their gaze should be different and what, exactly, it portended. *Nada malo, mija,* Delilah's abuela whispered in the wind. *At least, I hope nothing bad.* But Delilah did not find Abuela's tone convincing.

Gardens Like *Bajadas*

Afterwards, when Dolores and Abuela were living in the tiny house Abuela had moved into once her first set of children were grown and her last husband dead, people tended to forget that they hadn't always lived there together. Or they acted like they had forgotten. Abuela encouraged this by refusing to speak of her daughter, the husband, that night. Dolores was not to ask questions. Dolores didn't want to forget her mother, but it seemed kinder to Abuela to play along. Pretend that it had never happened. It was safer. After all, Abuela was all Dolores had left. Even though they weren't to speak about it, for nights and nights, Dolores heard Abuela weeping for her baby. Dolores understood that her mama was Abuela's baby, but Dolores longed for her mother with a different kind of want.

Dolores and Abuela huddled together through the rest of the winter and then spring. Abuela even took Dolores out of kindergarten, or rather, she just never sent the child back and no one came to ask why. They all knew why, really. Spring turned into summer. Dolores could start school over again in the fall, Abuela said. For now, she needed the girl close. But in the fall she didn't go back either.

Eventually, the phone rang and a meeting was arranged. Abuela dressed in her going-out clothes, dressed the child as if for church (if they'd ever gone to church) and they walked to the elementary school. Dolores heard Abuela and the principal of the school discussing the situation – Abuela in very polite Spanish and the principal lady in halting, grammatically imperfect Spanish that Abuela graciously pretended to understand – until she placed her palms over her ears and hummed. Finally, Abuela took Dolores's wrist and led her away, out of the office and the building. By then, the principal and her staff were already looking at them funny.

When spring came, Abuela rose at dawn and took Dolores into the garden. The front garden they mostly just maintained: trimmed the roses and the greenery, reseeded with the seeds Abuela had carefully saved when the annuals had started to fade, and watered nearly every day due to the dry desert wind. 'But not the succulents, *mija*. They prefer to be neglected.' The pair, dressed in the matching aprons Abuela sewed for them, sun hats and gloves, worked the front garden in the early mornings to avoid interacting with the neighbors who wanted to 'chat'.

'*Chismosa*,' Abuela would whisper through her false teeth when the woman from across the street walked off, stymied by Abuela's ability to smile charmingly while giving away nothing. The whistle at the end of 'gossiper' made the wispy hairs on Dolores's scalp and neck tingle. Despite the pleasure of the tingling, Dolores preferred people to stay away; their questions upset Abuela for hours afterwards. She hated seeing Abuela upset – it hurt her. To avoid the neighbors, they spent most of their time in the garden behind the house.

That garden was screened from outsiders' view by the tall cypress that Abuela had planted when Dolores's mama was young, interspersed with the citrus that grew so well in the dry, hot air. Here, their gardening ran wild. Abuela loved color and she loved fragrance, and she loved ignoring whatever rules said you couldn't plant purple bougainvillea next to orange poppies and marigolds, with scarlet daylilies thrusting their trumpet heads between them all. Roses planted at their bases climbed the trees, so pink-skinned grapefruit nestled next to white Lady Banksia blossoms spilling their petals onto Dolores's black braids below. Herbs for cooking and healing or getting rid of bugs; Abuela's lush *hierba de cucaracha* was given pride of place, sprawled on the ground where boring people ('We are many things but we are not boring, *mija*,' Abuela would say) grew patchy, nasty Bermuda grass. Abuela hated lawn. Lawn was for gringos.

Interspersed with the flashy colors of the plants exotic to the area were the more subdued colors, and often more intense scents, of the native plants. Dolores loved the olive-toned leaves of the brittle bush frosted with finger-staining white dust as much as she appreciated its lacy yellow flowers in the short spring. Abuela taught her to carefully harvest the tiny, five-leaved flowers of the wild borage they'd transplanted, wrapping the entire plant – roots, stems and thick, juicy leaves – in a dampened handkerchief when they'd found it growing in an abandoned park at the edge of a nearby *bajada*. The treasures that grew in these plains at the base of the mountain were worth more than gold to Abuela. Dolores preferred the deep purple of the cultivated European borage they'd stolen – er, clipped – from the garden of the man on the rich side of town, who owned a television factory on 'the other side' and spent most of his money on plants ordered from catalogues and cared for by a team of gardeners. All these gardeners were from Abuela's neighborhood, knew her, and carefully looked the other way should they happen to see her secateurs appear from her roomy pocketbook. Dolores was very careful never to mention her preference for purple in front of Abuela – or ever, in fact – because Abuela loved the native plants of her youth with a deep possessive force. Abuela defended what was hers.

Maybe it was her love for the native plants that caused her hatred of lawns, or maybe it was the waste. Why keep grass with water that should nourish the vegetables growing in pots on the small porch, or trickle through the rocks in the tiny pond on the shady side of the house? The pond was a luxury built when they found an abandoned aquarium left out with the trash on a rich man's street. By the time Abuela and Dolores were through digging the aquarium into the ground, and surrounding it with moisture-loving plants and stones selected on their walks, it looked like Mother Nature herself had designed it.

Their evening walks were taken when other families were eating dinner. Not only did they avoid well-meaning questions (and others not so well-meaning), but there were fewer eyes then to see the occasional scavenging of aquariums, or the more frequent pinching of cuttings or seed collecting that were the real aims of Abuela's nightly strolls. What little money there was went to food and shelter, and the twice-yearly shoes Dolores needed. Gardening was expensive, but gardening was what kept Abuela and Dolores from despair that first, terrible year. Gardening was their life, nurturing growth their solace.

They worked in the garden until their bellies rumbled for breakfast, and after eating, they worked until lunch and afternoon naps. In the evening, after their walk, they sat on the steps of the small house and planned for the next day. Before bed, Dolores would wrap her arms around her grandmother's waist and fiercely hug her.

'I love you,' Dolores said every night as she had said to her mama when her mama had tucked her into bed, one last kiss still moist on her soft baby cheek.

Dolores knew her grandmother loved her too, but Abuela never said the words back. She'd pat and soothe her bereft grandchild, then retire to her own room and weep for her dead daughter. But Dolores never lost hope that one night, Abuela would kiss her and say her words of love out loud.

*

When not in the garden, Abuela taught Dolores to keep house. Every day the floors were swept, the furniture dusted and the bathroom scrubbed. Once a week, the walls were washed and the old, clanking refrigerator was cleaned out and bleached. Laundry was washed and hung to dry on the back porch – '*Nunca, pero nunca*, where the neighbors may see your chonies, *mija*.' Never ever let the neighbors view your laundry – clean or otherwise.

Clothing, towels and bedding were mended until mending wasn't an option; then items were ripped into rags. Eventually, rags were sewn into strips of multi-colored cloth and the strips crocheted into rugs. Nothing was wasted, nothing was thrown out. Kitchen scraps were composted unless it was verifiable garbage, and that was placed into brown paper grocery bags – procured from the one grocery store Abuela frequented on the safe side of town, where Dolores was forced to use her Spanish or go unacknowledged – that were taken on their evening stroll and disposed of in a public refuse container.

'Just in case...' Abuela would say darkly.

Nunca, pero nunca was trash disposed of in front of a man in uniform or a sheriff's car or *la migra* or a car containing any man who looked 'official' and was driving by. If any of those appeared or Abuela abruptly noticed them, she turned on the Cuban heel of her lace-up shoes and walked them straight home, clutching Dolores's hand in hers the entire way. Once home, she locked all the doors behind them. The bag of trash was placed under the kitchen sink until the next day's walk, the shades were pulled, and the child bathed and put to bed. Then Abuela sat in her chair and sewed or mended or crocheted, and her lips worked as furiously as her fingers. The whispered words hissed out in an unending stream, not quite unintelligible to the child hiding and listening, but as constant as the sun and the drying wind of the town they lived in. Abuela wasn't praying; Dolores knew that, as she spied on her grandmother from the cracked-open bedroom door. Dolores knew Abuela wasn't praying even before she was taught to be wary of the men dressed in a uniform like her father used to wear, before he disappeared the night he murdered her mother.

Abuela didn't need to warn Dolores to stay away from the men in uniform, the men in official cars; Dolores had been afraid of men who looked like her father – whether the uniform or the expression, the body language or the smell – since before the night her father made her an orphan. Abuela didn't *need* to warn Dolores, but she did it every time anyway. She couldn't not do it. It was part of the same ritual of locking the doors, cleaning the house, hiding the trash and cursing the man who killed her daughter. Wherever that murderer had disappeared to, whoever had helped him, Abuela cursed them all.

The Golden Bed

When Delilah opened the door to the cottage for the first time, all she saw was a green glass hurricane lantern standing on a wicker table. It was dusk, and a late beam of winter sun caught the glass of the globe, creating a perfect starburst of color. The lantern, on its unsteady perch, was in the exact correct spot to be bumped with a hip and dashed to the floor, where it would shatter into a mess of spring-green shards and flammable lamp oil. Delilah stepped forward to move it to the floating mantel on the stone fireplace, and that was when the smell hit her.

It wasn't the mildewed, dusty, stale air of a house sealed up for the winter in a salt-wet clime. Well, it was that, but it was also the smell of something dead. The cottage contained a rotting animal, and Delilah was going to have to find it before she did anything else. The doors were shut behind her and the odor, stronger now, gagged her. She pivoted back, opened the door and screen, realized they needed to be blocked open and dragged a chair into the doorway to do so. She made a mental note to invest in a doorstop and get rid of the time-rotted chair. She stepped further back from the odor, walked into the garden and then the drive, taking deep breaths of sea air clean with salt, sucking in the breeze green with marsh grass – and was that bread baking? She took one more deep breath, filling her lungs with clean air, and then she made her way back to her new front door.

The stench once more gagged her, and Delilah's priorities shifted. First she would open every door and window in the house, and then she would find the dead thing. As her hard-soled penny loafers gritted across the wood floor, she added a new broom to her mental shopping list, and some orange oil and floor wax. All the living room windows were now open and Delilah moved to the kitchen. The smell intensified. As she raced to open the back door and screen, she held her breath. The window over the sink was warped or painted shut, or perhaps both. It wouldn't budge, so she opened the window facing the shared driveway – an aspect of the property the real-estate listing had not advertised – and ran from the room. Hopefully, the air would clear as she inspected the upstairs.

Oh, the upstairs! Delilah had never seen so much junk crammed into a house before, and her abuela was no slouch in the junk-collecting department. One bedroom, surely intended as the master since it was half again as large as the other, held two sets of bunk beds, an armoire that looked like it had been used for archery target practice, a large dresser with half its drawer pulls missing, and an old-fashioned washbowl and pitcher stand in the corner, next to the closet. The bowl didn't match the pitcher, and the fact that she even noticed this made Delilah laugh until the room's collection of ugliness shocked her into quiet. For a moment, she was overwhelmed by the sheer amount of work needed to make the cottage habitable. She shook off the feeling of oppression and opened the four windows.

The smaller room looked over what Delilah thought of as the back garden, but that was now merely a resting place for a broken barbecue, a leaning laundry line and dilapidated beach chairs. This room stood directly above the kitchen. The death odor was worse in here. A double mattress in an old iron-pipe bedframe was pushed into the corner. Another battered dresser, this one with a spotted and worn mercury mirror, stood against the far wall. There was a matching bedside table and to Delilah, no doubt light-headed from the stench and from holding her breath for so long, the dresser seemed overly proud of this distinction. She opened both windows and fled. She wouldn't realize until later that the smaller room was without a closet.

The only room left upstairs, beside the cramped hallway running its length, and also holding shadowy bits and pieces of miscellaneous furniture, was the lone bathroom. There was one fairly large window. *It must face the neighbor on the other side*, Delilah thought. The one with whom she did *not* share a driveway. Alan was going to throw a tizzy over the driveway, she just knew it. The bathroom was on the opposite side of the cottage from the yellow house, she was sure now, although she was a bit turned around in the stinky gloom. The window was covered by some ancient, filthy, matchstick blinds, their strings so frail with age and years of sun damage that when Delilah gave them the tiniest of yanks, they fell with a crashing cacophony into the claw-footed bathtub below. There was a cloud of dust and dirt, and the window glass was of course also foul, but Delilah was not so blinded that she didn't see the wizened face, in the window of the house next door, staring into hers.

Delilah let out a terrified scream and dropped to the floor. But it was covered with dust from the blinds and with grit from who knew how many years of feet, and she could feel the sand under her linen-covered knees (she hadn't bothered to change from her respectable traveling suit to her work overalls, so distracted was she by the dirty house and its smell of death), besides which, what must her poor old-lady neighbor think of her? Delilah's fear of the woman's appearance was terribly rude.

So she stood up, prepared to mime: 'Apologies, hello, hope I didn't scare you as much as you just did me.' But the window was empty, the shades drawn. For as long as Delilah lived in the cottage, her neighbor's window stayed that way.

There was a sign on the wall in the bathroom, a carved wooden plaque inlaid with shell lettering, which Delilah removed and eventually rehung in the kitchen after she'd painted the walls there flat white with apple-green trim on the wainscoting. She approved of the message the plaque imparted, but its place was not in the bathroom. In there the sign lacked dignity. In the kitchen it would encourage her each morning as she boiled water for her French press. *You are not obligated to complete the work, but neither are you free to abandon it.*

The cottage was not what Delilah had been expecting. She knew it had been shut up for a while, she knew it had been a rental, but she'd never known people could be so disgusting. Obviously, no one had cleaned the house before locking the doors and mailing the keys to the agent. The bedsheets were slept on, the trash wasn't emptied, and the smell? Dear God, the smell wasn't a dead animal as she'd originally thought. The smell was rotten bologna, rancid cheese and some sludge that might have begun its existence as iceberg lettuce. All this had been left in the icebox in a corner of the kitchen. Delilah wept as she cleaned up the mess; they were tears of rage, and the rage was aimed at herself.

Because, really, what did she expect? Did she think it was going to be easy? Was anything ever handed to you picture-perfect? This was a big, nasty mess, yes. But under it was Delilah's house, and she was going to make it beautiful. The harder you worked for something, the more you appreciated it, Abuela always said. Delilah was going to appreciate the hell out of this cottage, eventually. She raised her eyes to heaven and apologized to Abuela for blaspheming, even if only in her thoughts. Never mind that

Abuela was the one who had taught her to do so. *Do as I say, et cetera*; Abuela had waved a negligent hand to excuse her cursing in front of her granddaughter. Delilah wiped her eyes with the inside edge of her blouse, sniffed the rest of her tears away and got back to work.

Miraculously, there was a tiny, stackable washing machine and dryer in the kitchen so Delilah was able to wash some linen for a makeshift bed, but she couldn't stomach the smell of the little bedroom, and the eeriness of the bunk beds in the larger room gave her the cold gruesomes. There was a divan in the living room that wasn't too hideous. A wooden frame held a brown bouclé body-length cushion that was removable. This she dragged across the newly swept floor and out the kitchen door, where she threw it over a railing and beat the daylights out of it with the broom handle. Luckily, it was full dark by then so she couldn't see the clouds of dust rising, but after her coughing fit she knew they were there.

It was while pausing, waiting for the coughing attack to abate, that she noticed the lights in the house next door. Someone was moving from room to room right above her driveway. She couldn't hear footsteps or voices or music, but the lights turned on and off as the man (the solid shadow of the body blocking the too-strong electric light screamed *man*) walked through the house. Only a man would drink coffee – *strong* coffee if she could smell it from across the driveway – at this time of night. For no discernable reason, this movement, his existence, his scent, made Delilah nervous. The hair stood up on her arms. The house had looked abandoned earlier in the daylight, and she had thought it empty. She had thought wrong. The dusk quickly turned to dark and Delilah went inside to make what ablutions, and find what rest, she could. Disappointment was exhausting.

The next morning, after cleaning the kitchen and the bathroom, and sweeping all the floors, Delilah sat on the back-porch steps, drinking oily, milk-less coffee made from a stale jar of instant she'd found on a shelf and breakfasting on the leftovers from a package of cookies she'd bought on the ferry. She'd gotten little sleep in her bed of raggedy sheets on the floor next to the sooty fireplace (she was not going to think about *Cenicienta*), but she was full of a strange, anxious energy. There was so much to be done to make the cottage match the mental image she held of all that it could be.

Delilah, when looking at the photographs in the real-estate brochure and later on, while packing her belongings for the ferry ride, had imagined a cottage needing work, needing care and cleaning, but she had underestimated the depth of neglect she'd encounter. In her mind, the cottage was empty, open: white-painted walls waiting for her to add vibrant color. There would be wood or tile floors that needed a sweep or polish at the most, and nude windows waiting for her to add sheer curtains allowing in all the blue-toned island sunlight. She'd imagined the cottage a blank canvas waiting for her school of art – other artists painted or sculpted or baked or wove; Delilah was a master of homemaking and gardening. The cottage would be her artwork, yes, but it wasn't the empty canvas she'd expected. Some other vision had waited here for her: ugly linoleum, monstrous furniture, dirt-encrusted blinds marring every window and that nasty mess in the refrigerator. Delilah would scrape it all away and start anew; she had the skills. She could do it – she would do it – but for one moment she allowed herself to mourn the picture she'd envisaged. *Where would comfort come from...* (Abuela whispered Delilah's least favorite *consejo* into her ear where she sat on the steps) *...if it wasn't for the pain? Now get up and get to work.*

Delilah had a severe case of bed head, and her hair was falling in her face. In trying to smooth it or at least shove the worst of the mess behind her ears, she noticed the curtains at an upstairs window of the yellow house next door – the same window as last night's light-and-shadow show – twitch closed. Someone was watching her. Was someone always going to be watching her? Would she always be an object to be looked at? She had never understood those statues in a garden that served no purpose other than to be pretty. Delilah breathed deeply, once and again, closer to anger than resignation, before she stood up and went inside.

But in the kitchen, she read the sign on the wall about one's obligations, smiled to herself and thought, *No. I don't think so. I think I'm going to inspect that garage.* She would not be intimidated. She would not be swayed from her path. She might not be required to finish the work, but neither should she allow the gaze of others to stymy her. She had the right to live as she wanted. Delilah performed what morning ablutions she could with water heated on the stove, before she changed into her work clothes, pulled her uncombed hair into a ponytail and marched outside. The back garden was a hideous conglomeration of trash that needed to be disposed of, but she didn't have that tingly feeling of being watched anymore. Secure in her attitude of righteous indignation, she was a little disappointed. Oddly, for the first time in her life, she felt like a fight.

The garage's sliding door needed oil, but the roof was intact and one wall was covered in shelves. Old, dirty, cobwebby shelves that Delilah would use for storage. The building was musty and cold, and its sandy floor crunched underfoot; if there was pavement under there, years of blowing beach sand had long ago covered it. It was a sad, dismal edifice, full of unwanted things. A stack of comic books was disintegrating on one shelf; a rusty bicycle leaned against another. This dark, detached building was where generations of island renters had put items best forgotten, but not yet sufficiently old, broken or unwanted to be thrown away. Delilah was delighted. She owned a box containing such mementoes, items so unwanted she didn't like to sleep near them – this was the box's new home. On her way out the door, she took the stack of comic books. It was Wonder Woman who stared up at her – legs in battle stance, fists on hips – not Superman. Delilah hadn't read *Wonder Woman* in years.

'Back to work, Cinderella,' Delilah directed herself; then she coughed from the disturbance of the dust of the building and the comic books in her arms. Even the dust was disturbed by her. She smiled.

A man wearing nothing but red shorts and old running shoes was heading up the path to the driveway and looked at her, startled by her voice. By her presence. Their eyes met briefly before jerking away in heated reaction. He was sweaty, swarthy, not-quite-handsome-but-close, and seemed frightened by her existence. Delilah stepped back into the gloom of the garage once more, giving him time and an excuse to pass by without conversing. She'd never scared anyone before. It was so new and – yes, she admitted it – pleasing in its feeling of power that she tingled a little, before smiling again at her silliness. She dumped the comics back on the shelf where she'd found them. After all, she didn't have the time or inclination to reminisce. She passed a little more time by taking mental stock of any tools she could use. Besides the bicycle, it was mostly junk.

After visiting the garage, Delilah realized she would need proper tools before being able to proceed with home repairs. Sharp tools, perhaps power tools – tools that could double as weapons. It would be nice to sleep in a bed again someday, and that would require manual labor and much cleaning. She tried to imagine Alan's face should he be expected to join her on the makeshift mattress on the swept but still gritty floor.

'It would be funny,' she told the empty room. She knew Alan would not think so. She walked to the village stores. Time to meet the neighbors.

Island Hardware was fairly empty, but it was early in the day. A middle-aged lady stood behind the thick wooden counter, adding up receipts. She stopped and stared at the new customer. Delilah did not approach her, merely stared back. She thought it best to let the proprietor set the tone. Thus far, the tone was awkward. Delilah didn't know how to break the silence. The lady's stare was startled, accusatory and rather embarrassed. Delilah didn't like it at all.

'Thompson!' The woman didn't break eye contact as she called out.

From the stacks of towering merchandise, a tall, stooped man appeared, his eyebrows raised at his lady. The eyebrows went higher and then lowered when he spied Delilah standing there, the letter of introduction from Alan's bank in her hand.

'Oh,' the man said. 'Yup. Can I help you?'

'Is there such a thing as a chainsaw that doesn't run on gasoline?' Delilah gestured delicately with the letter as she spoke. 'I want to use it inside the house. But I worry about fumes.'

This was inherently not the question the man, Thompson, was expecting, for his eyebrows shot up again. Simultaneously, Delilah and the man realized they were both wearing overalls and black rubber boots. They matched. This relaxed them. Thompson's eyebrows attained normal altitude. Delilah didn't smile, in order not to irritate the still-watching woman. But she wanted to.

'I can order you a chainsaw that uses electricity,' Thompson said. 'But I think what you need is a circular saw, and I have one in stock you can take with you.'

'Do you deliver?' Delilah asked. She spread her hands for emphasis. 'Because I need to make a big order.'

The woman, Mrs Thompson, seemed rather more approving after hearing Delilah's news. Her arms dropped from her cross-clench and her stance relaxed. She took the pencil from behind her ear and held it with the eraser poised over her adding machine. She was ready.

'Yup,' Thompson said. 'We deliver.'

He beckoned her to follow him into the stacks, but Mrs Thompson waved Delilah over to the counter. Delilah, understanding which side her bread was buttered on in the hierarchy of women, walked to her. She held out her pencil-less hand for Delilah's letter and Delilah set it on the woman's open palm.

'When you're done,' Mrs Thompson said, 'you can use the telephone to call and have your own service started. Well, gracious,' she said after she read the letter. 'I'll do it for you while you shop. Then, in the future, you can just call in an order and we'll deliver it. Save you the need to come in.'

Thompson cleared his throat as he beckoned once more for Delilah to follow him. She thought about thanking Mrs Thompson, but decided against it when she realized the woman's offer meant she didn't want Delilah in her shop. Alan's money would be thanks enough. It the future, Delilah decided, she'd smile when she felt like it and only when she felt like it, whether this Mrs Thompson liked it or not.

The order was indeed so large that Mr Thompson called in a younger man – Thompson Junior, Delilah christened this one – to help load and deliver it. Delilah declined Junior's offer of a lift home in the cab; she needed to visit the greengrocer. She gave the proprietor there another bank letter in exchange for a wheeled wicker basket of staples and a paltry number of fresh vegetables. Delilah could see she would need to grow her own produce; thus, her entire garden plan would need to change. This challenge delighted her. Plans for an enlarged garden kept her mind occupied and blind to whatever attention she attracted, until she reached her driveway and discovered the Island Hardware truck was already unloaded. They'd put it all on the porch, but at her request they carried it into the living room. She hadn't locked any doors, but apparently island men didn't try doorknobs. Being inside made them visibly nervous and they departed before Delilah could say anything other than, 'Thank you.'

She got back to work. After she put the groceries away, she went upstairs and took her new circular saw to the ramshackle bunk beds. They were unfinished pine, so she stacked the wood neatly next to the fireplace. Delilah would have a fire next to her pallet that night. If she couldn't move an item of furniture, she'd take it apart with the electric drill that Thompson had sold her. If she couldn't take it apart, she'd cut it up with the saw. Delilah felt she was developing a real knack for controlled destruction.

She met no one else except for the telephone installation man. An obvious off-islander, he was inclined to be overly friendly, until Delilah fired up her circular saw and cut the old wooden icebox to bits. He cleared off quickly when the sawdust flew.

When her home was once again hers, she cleaned up the mess of the chopped-apart icebox – sweeping and mopping the hardwood floor after stacking the wood and metal hardware on the back porch – and then picked up the receiver of the new white plastic wall telephone.

At Island Hardware, Mrs Thompson answered. Delilah identified herself politely and waited for a response.

'Uh-huh,' Mrs Thompson said.

'I need a refrigerator,' Delilah said. 'What's the smallest you have?'

There was a considerable pause. In the blank noise of the open phone line, Delilah couldn't judge the tone of Mrs Thompson's silence. Was she still there?

'Hello?'

'The smallest is just a little one for offices and such,' Mrs Thompson finally said. 'We have none in stock, and I don't think that's what you want.'

Her tone now was grudgingly interested, but then *Who doesn't love new appliances?* Delilah reasoned. She hopped up on the permanently sticky kitchen counter (so far she hadn't found a cleanser strong enough to remove whatever residue resided there), the better to enjoy the chat.

'Plus, there's no freezer in those little ones.' Mrs Thompson definitely disapproved of a refrigerator without a freezer, that much was clear.

'No, no,' Delilah said, although she was agreeing. 'Not like that. I want a small refrigerator with a small freezer.'

'You could also get a separate deep freeze,' Mrs Thompson said. 'That's what everyone does. Keep a separate freezer for winter when sometimes we're cut off. It's a precaution.'

'This kitchen doesn't have much room,' Delilah found herself apologizing to Mrs Thompson. She scraped at a lurid stain in the grout with a thumbnail.

'We keep ours in the garage,' Mrs Thompson said. 'The deep freeze. But also, we have a generator in case we lose power. Which happens also.'

Delilah paused. She felt warm, but surprised. She was confused by Mrs Thompson engaging in this conversation. Was this what people did, normally? Was the other woman enjoying their conversation, too? Perhaps she was merely trying to sell Delilah as many large, expensive appliances as possible, but it felt like a real exchange. Delilah was no longer accustomed to women being friendly – it had been a while. Since before she moved to the island, since before she moved in with Alan in the city apartment. Since before puberty. Since the age of five. Delilah was momentarily stricken, but she wasn't sure by what. She was no longer warm; in fact, she had goosebumps.

'Hello?'

'Yes, sorry.' Delilah coughed. 'Could you order the smallest standard-size refrigerator for me? Put it on my tab?'

'White, ivory or this new avocado?'

'White.'

'Oh good,' said Mrs Thompson. 'That avocado is awful.'

Delilah giggled. She hadn't giggled in ages, and it was more nerves than anything, but it was honest. Mrs Thompson was silent. Delilah stopped giggling. She'd never learned these rules. The goosebumps receded.

'It should be in next week,' Mrs Thompson said briskly.

'Thank you,' Delilah said, but the line was empty. Delilah stood with the receiver in her hand, her finger in the rotary dial. She wanted to call someone else. There was no one else to call. She shook off the feeling, whatever it was. Loneliness? She didn't have time for that. Confusion about Mrs Thompson's grudging, quasi-friendly conversation? Delilah wasn't sure she wanted to question what had just happened, but neither did she like the woman any better. Maybe she'd grow on Delilah. She thought of mistletoe, kudzu vine and moss hanging from swamp trees, and she shuddered. Maybe not.

Delilah preferred Mr Thompson, he of the 'yup' and the overalls and the appreciation of anyone willing to discuss the merits of a good chainsaw. When Delilah had asked him if he rented floor sanders, his eyes had filled with delighted wonder. He'd always wanted to, it turned out. But no one had ever asked. Mr Thompson wasn't scary at all. But then, Delilah knew how to handle the Mr Thompsons of the world. She'd been trained.

The front porch was cluttered again with Delilah's reject pile, so she called the local thrift shop. Once the thrift store promised to have the donations collected right away, Delilah used the new-smelling telephone to order linens and curtains and rugs from the Macy's on the mainland. She thought a moment, running through options in her mind, then ordered a queen-sized mattress, too. She put it all on Alan's account. They promised two-day delivery, so Delilah ripped up most of the existing sheets and towels to make cleaning rags.

She felt like she was under the gun, but what gun and whose she couldn't say. Delilah couldn't live in a dirty house, so she was cleaning it. She wouldn't live surrounded by ugliness, so she was beautifying it. Life should be comfortable. She justified the expense of it all by saying it was for Alan. She was making a nice home for Alan, but she knew this wasn't it. This space was her space, and she wanted it clean and spare and beautiful because when spring arrived and the garden called to her, Delilah wanted to be able to forget the house, leave the house, and answer the garden's call. When spring arrived and the garden needed her, Delilah would be ready.

She picked up the telephone again. The rotary dial made a satisfying burr as it clicked through the numbers. She held the receiver to her ear to better hear the hum of the lines connecting. The sound nuzzled into her ear like companionship.

'Island Hardware.'

'I forgot to ask you about paint,' Delilah said. 'I need gold paint.'

'Gold?' Mrs Thompson asked. 'Did you say gold?'

'Yup.' Delilah borrowed island vocabulary. 'Like the metal.'

'Um.' Mrs Thompson thought out loud. 'I think we have little tubes for craft projects.'

'No,' Delilah said. 'I need about a gallon. Paint for metalwork. Is that enamel? Maybe I should come in and talk to Mr Thompson.'

'That's not necessary,' Mrs Thompson snapped. Delilah wondered if the woman's professional pride was pricked or if this was some kind of wifely jealousy. 'I handle the paint inventory.'

Ah, professional pride. Delilah could understand that. She could approve of that.

'I will order you one gallon of gold enamel paint,' Mrs Thompson said. 'It might take a couple of days.'

'Okay,' Delilah said cheerfully. 'Thank you.'

Mrs Thompson dropped the telephone. Delilah heard it clatter before the dial tone started. She might eventually enjoy these little chats after all. It made for a nice break in her work routine.

The larger bedroom was finally emptied of furniture, and the iron bedframe from the smaller room was in pieces on the tarp-covered floor. Delilah was going to paint the frame a deep, rich gold. The iron bedframe would be a mockery of a big brass bed. She would rebuild it, piece by piece, in the master bedroom. Then, she would sleep in a real bedroom, in a real bed; no more pallet in front of the fire.

Delilah adjusted her ponytail, unclipped her overalls to tie the loosened top at her waist and eyeballed the changes to the kitchen one last time before she grabbed her toolbox with one hand and her electric drill with the other, and walked upstairs. 'You are not Cinderella,' she said out loud, firmly. 'You are Wonder Woman.'

Roots Like Monsters

When Dolores went back to kindergarten in the fall, starting over from the beginning, it was as if everyone had forgotten her existence. She didn't know her classmates, who – even though they were only a year younger than she – seemed especially babyish. The teacher and her aide tried to treat Dolores like just another little pigtailed girl in Mary-Jane shoes who liked to make daisy chains out of dandelions instead of playing hopscotch with the other girls, but Dolores felt their avid or pitying glances always on her. And Dolores was the only child the principal sent for once a week to drink milk from a cafeteria carton as the woman attempted to engage her in conversation.

Abuela told Dolores that her mama was nobody's business but theirs, and Mama had always told Dolores that if you can't say anything nice (or safe, in cases when Daddy was around), keep your mouth shut. *La lengua guarda al pescuezo, mija.* So during these weekly visits with the principal, despite the lady's kind eyes and gentle manner, Dolores drank her milk, eyed the woman's lacquered blonde beehive, and did her best to keep her mouth shut and her neck safe.

Unfortunately, Dolores's silence seemed to intrigue the principal even more. At first, they sat staring at each other once the lady ran out of questions or breath. The starkly white-painted room, redolent of cafeteria food cooking next door and a tang of cigarette smoke that the spray of Estée Lauder's Youth Dew couldn't hide, felt like a bright cage, but the silent staring contests didn't last. The next visit, alongside the carton of milk, there appeared a stack of large, stiff white cards with black ink splotches. Dolores eyed these with foreboding and refused to touch her milk.

'Now, child,' the principal said. 'I thought we'd play a game.'

Dolores sat back in the scarred wooden chair, her feet swinging several inches above the ground. She crossed her arms over her pinafore, protecting her soft belly. She didn't like games; she never had. People who wanted to play them were not to be trusted, in her experience. They said 'games' like both were playing, but only they were having fun. Dolores wanted to run. She pointed her toes so that they skimmed the floor and her arms uncrossed to grip the bottom of the hard chair. She was ready.

'I'll hold up these pictures, see?' The lady's voice was kind, but Dolores didn't trust it. *Even the devil can quote scripture*, Abuela would say. 'There is no right or wrong answer – it isn't that kind of game. You just tell me what you see.'

She held up the stack of cards so that the picture faced Dolores, who turned her head to stare into the adjacent bathroom, too dark for her to examine the tilework. Dolores would rather clean the grout than play whatever *tonteria* this lady was up to. The principal let the first card fall to her desk. It made a slight swish through the air and a soft thwack as it hit the surface. Dolores turned back. She liked the sound of the lady's defeat.

'That one isn't very interesting, is it?' The lady said brightly. 'Let's try the next.'

The next card looked very much like a dying spider plant to Dolores's eyes. Those were hard to kill – you'd have to neglect one for a long time to get it in that sad of a condition, drooping and forlorn. It most likely needed new soil or, at the very least, top-dressing. She was inadvertently interested; the principal picked up on this spark. Dolores did not like how the lady actually saw her, saw Dolores on the inside. It was not safe.

'What do you see, dear? Do you recognize this? Is it a person?'

That was so stupid, Dolores turned away again. A person! The roots of a spider plant were like thick, white, juicy worms, sucking the life from the soil around them, growing until they pushed free of their pot. The thin stripey green-and-white leaves were deceptively pretty, but really the plant was a hungry monster taking and taking until there was nothing left. A person? This woman was just silly. Dolores drank her milk after all – opening the carton and placing the straw just right gave her an excuse to avoid the principal. Let her hold up all the dead and dying plant paintings she wanted. Dolores wasn't a baby; she wasn't going to be tricked again.

The principal gave up and sent Dolores back to class, but over the next weeks the sinister cards gave way to word association games, hidden figure pictures from glossy magazines and audio tapes that sounded like the fuzz of a broken television to Dolores. Abuela said, 'The poor woman is obviously insane, *mija*. Just humor her and hopefully she'll eventually get bored.'

Dolores, accustomed to the vagaries of adults, heaved a put-upon sigh and prepared to deal with the principal once a week for what felt like the rest of her life. She didn't even like plain milk; would it kill the cafeteria to serve them chocolate milk? But Abuela was right – the principal got bored and gave up. She gave the original dying-plant cards to Dolores, who used the provided crayons to bring the plants back to vivid life. During their hour together, as Dolores finished a card, the principal would hang it on the corkboard behind her. Dolores still didn't understand the point of it all, but as long as the woman didn't question her and allowed her to save the plants on the cards, Dolores was able to relax for the brief time she spent in the principal's office. The rest of her day at school, not so much.

*

School made Dolores so nervous – the adults were always staring and the children always questioning – that every afternoon Abuela taught her a new skill to calm her down. A capable girl was a girl in control, Abuela counseled. A girl in control of herself was capable of anything. Eventually, Dolores would be that girl.

Having learned to mend and sew and crochet during Abuela's nightly cursing sessions, they moved on to light carpentry and painting. Taping off the windows and wainscotting soothed Dolores into an almost hypnotic state. The scent of the paint layered neatly over the washed walls didn't give her a headache but instead filled her with a sense of contentment. Room by small room, they repainted. Each finished room, sweetly scented and brand new through her labor, filled her with a sense of purpose. With a paintbrush in her hand, Dolores's life held meaning. When eight-year-old Dolores was capable of taping, tarping and painting on her own, Abuela moved on to upholstery.

That Dolores's favorite part was whacking the tacks in with her small hammer did not go unnoticed, and on her birthday (they'd stopped celebrating Christmas after *that* night; Abuela couldn't even bake cookies or put up a tree without sobbing), Abuela gave her her very own tiny, perfect tools in a pretty lacquered box. Knowing Abuela must have saved for months for the gift made Dolores appreciate it even more. Her grandmother had planned, and thought of her, for all that time.

Between painting, upholstery and of course their one true love, gardening, there was all the other upkeep demanded by an aging house. Abuela taught her to unclog a sink, a toilet and the bathtub drain; they rewired a lamp and regrouted the tiles in the shower wall. Dolores was likely the most skilled ten-year-old in the entire town, Abuela reckoned, and Dolores straightened her shoulders in pride.

Each skill conquered made her stand taller, hold her head high. So what if she had no friends? Could the little girls who didn't invite her to their birthday parties fix the electrical socket in their bedroom? Could the little boys who stared at her in the cafeteria while she ate her green beans all alone snake the bathtub when it clogged up with their thick, black hair?

Eventually, Dolores at thirteen was more knowledgeable about homemaking than most women when they first left their mother's home to be married. The only class at the high school that Abuela thought Dolores would eventually find useful was auto-shop, but girls weren't allowed and Abuela couldn't afford a car even if she knew how to drive one. Dolores would have to walk or take the one dusty bus that serviced the town until her grandmother could get her safely raised and out of it, Abuela told her.

The one goal Abuela held after the death of her youngest child and only daughter was to raise *her* daughter to be as self-sufficient as possible and to get her safely out of the godforsaken town that had taken Dolores's mother. Anything beyond competency, safety and escape was a bonus, as far as Abuela – and, by extension, Dolores – was concerned. They had no other ambition than survival. Whatever was done to achieve these goals – any action at all – was *justo*. Enough had been taken from them, Abuela taught, so whatever they took back was fair game and would never, *pero nunca*, compare to what they'd already given and what was owed them in return. Abuela would settle for survival. Dolores, at eight and ten and thirteen, was still on the fence.

Blue Hydrangea

There was one garden in particular on the island that Delilah admired. It was inland, away from the sometimes-rough wind of the coast, and just distant enough from the village proper that it took her a while to discover it on her swooping, unplanned, self-guided garden tour. This garden she found was so lushly perfect that she did a double take riding by, and made a U-turn before stopping her bicycle and dismounting: a high compliment. She was studying the plantings and the layout from the polite distance of the front gate when a man wearing mud boots came around the side of the house and spoke to her.

'Hello,' he said.

Delilah let go of the willow-weave garden gate and took a step back. She shouldn't touch what wasn't hers, but she hadn't expected anyone to be home. Even if she'd seen him, she wouldn't have figured he would speak to her. Islanders didn't speak to her. If she'd learned one rule since moving here, it was that. Those hydrangeas, though! Anyone who grew those was someone she could learn from. And he had spoken first. Maybe he followed different rules.

'Hello,' she said. It came out too softly. She cleared her throat. 'Hello. I was just admiring your hydrangeas.'

He smiled warmly and proudly. It was a gardener's smile; she recognized it plainly. This gave her the courage to go on.

'Might I ask...' she said, but then started over. 'My hydrangeas are sad specimens compared to these monsters. I'd be embarrassed for you to see them.'

'It's the soil,' he said. 'Your soil is too sandy over there, and I expect a little salty. Plus, the wind...'

Delilah stiffened. He knew where she lived? Who she was? *Calm down, mija. Small town, small island*, she reminded herself and relaxed. Perhaps all hydrangeas on the island were buffeted by salty breeze and malnourished by sandy soil. Maybe he alone held the cure. He looked old enough to know. *Old enough to know better*, Abuela whispered, but Delilah brushed her away. She liked this gardener's looks. He looked kind, a little sad, and there was dark, loose garden soil on his hands.

'Could I amend it?' she asked, her chin gesturing to his hands. 'The soil? Any advice?'

His eyes widened, but not in a surprised way. Delilah knew that look. She'd asked an older man to explain something to her, give his wise counsel. Inwardly, she sighed in resignation and relief. They were so easy. It was always so easy.

He opened the beautifully cared-for wicker gate to invite her into his garden. Up close he looked old enough to have fathered her. This didn't make her nervous, oddly – after all, she hadn't had the best luck with fathers, but something in this man's manner relaxed her. He was restful; his soul seemed calm. His hair was not blond, as she'd judged from a distance, but gray. Although most of the islanders past the age of twenty possessed crow's feet from squinting in the glare, he had more. The lines around his mouth looked like the residue of laughter, but laughter that had ended a while ago. He looked tired. He looked so sad.

Delilah sighed again. This resignation contained no relief. She was annoyed with her instincts now. She needed to remember to rein herself in.

He led her through his garden. They lingered by the hydrangeas massed against the front of his saltbox home, but she was entranced away by a wisp of an odor – spicy, exotic. 'What *is* that?' she asked, sniffing greedily, and his smile broadened as he showed her around back to his Cedar of Lebanon.

'So beautiful,' Delilah said, inhaling. She gazed up at the lacy branches and then back down to earth, studying the multi-hued green dappled by the branches' dancing shade. 'And so peaceful.'

Nothing was in flower yet – spring was so new – but Delilah knew her leaves and her greens, her trees and her shrubs. Her mind's eye saw what *was* and filled in what *would be*. There were silvery blue hosta, the black foliage of crape myrtle and specialized mallow, and the fiery orange-red of the native Carpinus caroliniana, but the variety of the green was equally spectacular. Here was the glossy deep magnolia, the dusty gray of a weeping blue atlas cedar – not as scented as the nearby Cedar of Lebanon, but fascinating with its contorted shape draped over a rotting split-rail fence slowly bowing to time and the growing cedar's weight. The shades and variations of green, highlighted by the specimen plants that were not green, looked more than natural. They looked supernatural: an Impressionist painting come to life. The garden was a masterpiece. This man was an artist. Delilah wanted to take his hand, acolyte-like, and kiss it. She stepped further away from him in consequence. She needed to remember her place.

'I spend most of my time here,' he said at that moment. 'Since my wife died, I don't seem to want to do much else.'

Delilah looked at him, quickly, up from her fingering of an Artemisia bush. Her eyes read his face, but she didn't speak. She didn't offer condolences. She remembered not wanting to hear them from others when it was her grieving. She remembered no solace then, except through gardening. The bitter scent of the crushed white leaves of the Artemisia swirled on the slight breeze that reached this far inland.

'This place gets all my attention,' he said when he must have realized she wasn't going to ask questions or offer any words of polite sympathy. She didn't know how to do that, not without revealing too much. 'That is, when I'm not working for the town.'

Delilah looked the question at him, rubbing the sprig of Artemisia she'd broken off the shrub over her closed lips. Little bits of dusty white no doubt dotted the unpainted pink of the mouth she now slightly opened. She should stop what she was doing, she knew that. This behavior was dangerous. But she didn't want to stop. The Artemisia reminded her of the brittle bush of her childhood, but nostalgia wasn't what tempted her now. He was in pain, and that pain called to her.

'I'm Ted. I'm the sheriff,' he told her, his eyes on her lips. He said it shyly, obviously not used to announcing his profession. Usually, it was known. As of course it would be on the island.

Delilah almost fainted.

Ted saw the girl's face pale and her body recoil, and he wondered at it. She jerked like she'd received an electric shock. The shock filled the air around them with a subtle scent of fear. Ted's mouth tasted like he'd inadvertently bitten into aluminum foil, and she grimaced as she swallowed the no-doubt bitter specks of Artemisia. Why should she fear him? Her living situation was perhaps immoral if you asked some of the island's old biddies, but it wasn't illegal. As Ted watched, her shock and the flash of fear were almost immediately suppressed. Her reactive control was so impressive and quick that Ted could have told himself he'd imagined it, but he didn't. He was old enough to be tired of those games and had been sheriff long enough to trust his hair-on-the-back-of-the-neck instincts. Human beings were always going to go further than one could previously have believed them capable of going. They were always going to disappoint you.

That's it, Ted thought. *She'll flee the interview and never return.* He'd only see her during the drive-bys he and his lone deputy made routine. He would never host her in his garden again, although maybe for his shrub's sake that was a good thing. She'd roughed up a branch of his Artemisia pretty good there. He realized the thought of never seeing her again in his garden's beauty made him sad, frustrated. And there it was, on cue – he was suffused with disappointment. *You're being ridiculous*, he rebuked himself sternly. She was a stranger; there was no expectation of friendship, and she was young enough that authority made her nervous.

Delilah stilled her panicked response to Ted's announcement. He was the sheriff; normal girls shouldn't feel faint upon learning of a nice man's profession. It was just a job, probably one he'd been elected to by the good people of the island. They must respect him, hold him in high esteem. There was nothing in his demeanor – *so far*, Abuela hissed – to indicate he was violent or angry or bad. Ted was calm; he had those sad eyes; he knew so much about hydrangeas. There was no reason Delilah's mouth should dry in fear, or her heart be beating loudly in her ears. This kindly man looked like he wanted to make her a sandwich, not like he meant her any harm.

He looked nothing like her missing father, nothing. And it wasn't that she had even thought that, of course, when Ted told her. Even then he'd been shy and sweet, announcing his position of authority – imagine! Her reaction, the jerk back, it reflected the shock her system took every time she saw a uniform. But he wasn't a wearing a uniform – he was dressed like a gardener. He dressed like *Delilah*, down to the grass stains on his knees. There was soil under his fingernails, not the skin of his victims.

Delilah delicately shook off her shock, starting at her neck and working down her arms through her fingers, star-fishing out at her sides. Ted shifted in response, brushing his palms on the sides of his faded gardening khaki trousers. Dust and bits of shredded mustard weed billowed out. How could Delilah fear someone who loved to nurture nature as much as she did? She couldn't. She took a deep breath of the beautifully loamy scent that surrounded them, and forced her body into serenity. This man wished no one harm.

Ted saw a strange thing. Delilah's posture changed once more. She took a deep breath, held it and then released it. Gone was the rigid control. She put the crushed sprig in her pocket and smiled up at Ted wryly. She looked embarrassed, shy. He was confused, but relieved. She was prettier than all his plants put together – more beautiful even than his prized, heirloom *rosa rugosa* that covered the trellis next to the screened porch. Then the girl said something that went straight to Ted's heart.

'What color are the hydrangea's flowers?'

'Blue,' he said. Her dark eyes lit up with joy. She smiled, and he smiled back at her pleasure.

As they strolled across the plush lawn behind his house to the kitchen garden, they discussed pH-balancing of the soil that turned the multi-flowered globes the deep cyanotic blue. Ted admitted that the lawn took more than its fair share of water, but he thought it was pretty. He overseeded it with clover, he told her. He thought the occasional heart-shaped leaf and tiny white-globed flower were even prettier, and the lawn was practically a cover crop that way. The girl's eyes smiled even as she looked disapproving. The word 'pretty' felt overt in Ted's mouth as he looked at her, and he felt the fierce blush staining his cheeks.

During his trips by her house, Ted watched as she developed her kitchen garden in the front. He understood her reasoning;

there was more room, more sun, a fence to use as garden bones. He still found it scandalous, yet also intriguing. Just like her.

There was a proper method of hanging laundry on a line, here on the island – still taught by mothers to daughters in these modern days of the 1970s. Private items of clothing went on the innermost lines, and sheets and towels on the outside; even clean laundry wasn't for public view. This girl had taken a circular saw to her laundry line out back and then burned the wood. But she planted the garden that supplied her food in full view of anyone passing. What more was she capable of? Ted had to wonder, as he showed her his kitchen garden hidden from all eyes but his own, at the back of his property, screened from the road. This was the proper placement of a vegetable bed to Ted's way of thinking, but he was careful not to share it with this iconoclast.

By the end of the tour, near the rows of baby cabbages and the silver-green leathery leaves of not-yet-flowering eggplants, he liked the girl. He was sorry she wouldn't be back, as he was still convinced she wouldn't be. He was old enough not to kid himself that her loveliness and her scent of honey mixed with freshly turned loam didn't add to her attraction. But mostly it was just nice to talk to someone as obsessed with gardening as he was. Ted admitted that after only one conversation, he would miss her. He should be embarrassed by that. He was not. And he loaned her his favorite book, his name printed boldly on the flyleaf, to cement their friendship. Even if she never came back, a part of him would be with her.

But she came back. It took a week, but she did.

Under her arm she carried the book on compost he'd loaned her, its edges now starry with bits of seed-packet paper she'd used as bookmarks, and some old issues of horticulture magazines. Ted was pleasantly surprised until he realized the slips of paper between the pages marked her notes; she wanted to discuss issues specific to the island's climate, soil and seasonal changes. She was coming to learn from him; astounded pleasure was drowned in a wave of mixed emotions so foreign that Ted feared to examine them. He plucked one from the loam, like weeding the garden, to focus on: he was honored she'd chosen him for advice. He was merely *excited* to find another avid gardener, someone who shared a like-minded dedication to the beauty of flora – it was an entirely respectable and completely socially acceptable response. As one of the most responsible members of island society, he had a duty of care to the young newcomer.

Nevertheless, Ted was very careful not to touch her when he invited her into the kitchen for a cup of tea and use of the table upon which to spread her notes; he held his arm in a semicircle far from her slender shoulders as he opened his door. He told himself he'd only imagined the flash of fear during her first visit: the flinch and recoil from him, the paling of her exertion-reddened cheeks before she recovered that placid equanimity that Ted found soothing and exciting (*no, not that, Ted*) in equal measure. He was a stranger then, after all. She was young and newly arrived from the city – being wary was wise.

'Do you have time for me?' Delilah asked today and it was Ted's turn to flush red.

'Absolutely, yes,' he said and she stepped across his threshold.

Her slight hesitation before she entered, he put down to a thorough wiping of her sneakered feet on his hedgehog shoe-brush. *Someone raised her right*, Ted thought, but thinking of who that might be – possibly his contemporary in age – gave him another potting-soil-sized bag of mixed emotions. His thoughts shied away to the more mundane recollection of how to treat a guest. It had been a while.

He made tea and served scones given to him by his deputy's mother. Since his wife's death, the sheriff had taken for granted such gifts from the island's womenfolk, especially the spinster or widowed ladies of a certain age, and he barely noticed when the gifts of baked goods slacked off shortly after the girl's third visit.

The third time she arrived unannounced, Ted blurted, 'Did you have a telephone installed?'

Delilah only smiled and showed him her offerings of thick drawing paper and a vinyl bag of colored pencils, glossy and fresh as an island sunrise.

'I'm learning to draw garden plans,' Delilah said in that low, dark voice like freshly turned soil. 'Would you mind if I practiced on yours?'

Ted told himself once again that the feeling flooding him was honor. He was honored she'd chosen him, his garden. The pleasure in her company, her obvious assumption that he'd join her, was an added bonus. Ted blushed, then laughed in chagrin at his blush. Two gardeners enjoying their passion together – what could be more neighborly?

'May we sit there?' Delilah pointed at the white wrought-iron table and chairs that Ted's wife had bought, which he'd always considered useless frou-frou.

With overalled Delilah sitting at the table, implements of her art spread out, black-haired head bent studiously down as she patiently traced boundary outlines, Ted saw the setting as exactly right. The chairs had found their use. All that was missing was the tea and orange-marmalade muffins served in the same covered basket they'd arrived in that morning. Ted joined Delilah under the arborvitae, shaded by the deliciously scented Cedar of Lebanon, and poured her a cup of tea before taking up paper and grass-green pencil, and applying himself to the task his visitor had set him.

*

It was a beautiful day without wind, and many people out walking and biking witnessed their sheriff and the girl engaged in... whatever mysterious activity they were engaged in. Their heads were bowed over the paper-covered table and they passed the colored pencils back and forth. Whatever it was, it looked intimate.

'Drawing?' Mrs Oakapple asked her great-niece Maud when she called to pass along what she'd witnessed on her walk. Maud was a vigorous walker, if not quite a near neighbor of the sheriff. 'You mean like artistic drawing?'

'Like coloring,' Maud said. 'Mm-hm. I saw the pencils roll off the table and no one bothered to pick up the mess.'

'Drawing,' Mrs Oakapple said, at a loss for words. 'I'll be...'

She sat back in her elderly chair, squashed into the exact shape of her barely padded brittle bones, and stared out of her front window onto the street. Coretta Oakapple, who had never owned a television – merely a telephone and connections to virtually every soul (living and dead) on the island – was at the age where she thought people were no longer capable of surprising her. But now she had this new neighbor, so much more *active* than the man in the yellow house. She had heard even he showed signs of keeping tabs on the girl.

Maybe he wasn't so sinister after all. Mrs Oakapple tried to adjust her thinking the day she heard them exchanging pleasantries (or shouting – she wasn't sure which, with her hearing), but then again, the girl was young and lovely and no better than she should be. *No*, Mrs Oakapple decided, *he's a man and therefore most likely up to no good.*

'But drawing,' Coretta marveled. 'The girl has the sheriff drawing.'

The island got its share of visiting artists every summer, of course – its rugged beauty and convenient ferry saw to that. But the sea wind buffeting the coast and the grass-covered dunes high enough to offer excellent perspective also meant that the occasional blast sent easel, paint and canvas flying – oftentimes it was all caught up in a vortex and went backwards into the sea. Mrs Oakapple blessed the geographically odd winds that kept her home from being even more polluted with outsiders than it already was. 'After all,' she said darkly, 'look what happened to Nantucket.'

But that the sheriff was taking up with her neighbor girl – here was a puzzle. Whether it blew an ill wind or fair was a matter on which she reserved judgment. As she prepared to deploy her watchers, she felt a flutter of… something… in her blood. No doubt she needed to check her sugar levels, but Mrs Oakapple also recognized – because pragmatism had defined her nature even when she was growing in her mother's womb – that the trouble brewing in the sheriff's garden and whatever was happening in the yellow house down the street was causing the flutter she felt. Mrs Oakapple, oldest person on the island, was still alive and the flutter in her blood was interest.

A storm was brewing on the island; the pressure was growing; her army of lady auxiliaries was preparing; and Coretta Oakapple was very interested in what would be left once it had all blown up and over. Storms frequently left treasure, as well as destruction, in their wake.

'Drawing,' she said one final time before dialing Maisie Thompson at the hardware store. 'These things start out so innocent.'

Normally, the sheriff was attuned to the general mood of the citizenry; a man in his position had to be. When the food baskets stopped, however, he barely questioned it. The women no longer feeding him – well, maybe there was an etiquette-sanctioned cut-off date for the feeding of widowers. The attitude of the men he really should have seen, he thought later. He had no excuse. Men of his generation became almost respectful in an odd, envious manner. Men of a younger generation, the girl's generation, were one step away from hostile. These men took their speeding or parking tickets, their warnings about loud music at the beach, the confiscation of their open bottles of alcohol, with resentment muffled by years of ingrained respect for his station.

The sheriff should have noticed all this and drawn conclusions, and perhaps addressed the issue, but he didn't. By the time the women stopped feeding him completely – the baked goods ended first; the casseroles trickled gradually to a stop because the island's thrifty housewives found them a convenient way to dispose of leftovers that their own picky men didn't want to eat – he was sleeping with the girl when she came to talk gardens. When men his age paid him the dubious compliment of envy, he was already in love with her. Even if he had realized the young men were taking the tickets from his hand with contemptuous resentment because he'd dared to do what none of them had – and succeeded – it wouldn't have mattered. It was too late.

After a while, the sheriff's garden was no longer picture-perfect. In fact, the edges were distinctly raggedy. Sometimes plants were actually wilting before he watered them. He didn't notice that either, so busy was he – so obsessed – with tending to the girl and, by extension, to her garden. He'd have been amazed by any accusations of seduction. He'd had no such intention.

It was a very wet spring, the roads were muddy and Delilah had no car. She wore her overalls and mud boots to his house. Another thing he should have noticed from the beginning: she discouraged him from visiting her cottage. He'd never been inside. He'd cruise by on patrol and eyeball her garden; he felt he knew each plant as a friend, but only because of her detailed garden plan. He'd never walked in her garden.

It was softly raining again that day, the first day they were truly together. She arrived on her bicycle. Her floppy rain hat and yellow slicker kept her from being sopping, but her boots were muddy and the legs of her overalls were dark with moisture. She looked more than uncomfortable. She reminded Ted of a cat he'd fished from the lagoon after a tourist's boating accident, the creature too miserable to bare its claws. Ted waved Delilah solicitously into the mudroom before he took her hat and coat.

When he turned away for the towel he kept warming over the radiator for just such a purpose, he heard the clasps on her overalls click open. He turned back right as she stepped from her clothing, easy as breathing. She placed the wet denim on the radiator and gave Ted a moment to collect the emotions he was not accustomed to feeling, much less displaying. Ted didn't have the vocabulary to describe the sensations Delilah caused to course through his bloodstream like an unmapped watershed. He held those sensations inside, close to his breast, like a small dam pooling precious stream water. Delilah tilted her face up in order to smile directly at him, into his eyes, and what he had collected broke through his defenses and flowed freely once more.

She still wore her long-sleeved cotton shirt; this one was pink, faded by the sun, and came to mid-thigh. It was a man's shirt, but nothing her city boyfriend would have ever worn, or at least, that was what Ted chose to believe. Her thick socks were the color of brown-sugared oatmeal. One foot rested upon the other as she waited for him to invite her into the kitchen. Ted was pretty sure that everything he could see was all she was wearing. He cleared his throat and invited her through the door with one arm out in welcome. 'Get inside, come in.'

'You're probably cold,' he said, because he couldn't stop talking. 'I'll make tea.'

She sat at the table, still toweling her hair. She'd undone her braid, and the damp length of it curled as it dried. They drank the tea while looking over her newest garden plan. The back garden's emptiness was exciting her, she told him. She licked the sweetness of the honey he'd added to her cup from her lips. This plan, her latest, was still in its infancy, but there was so much nothing to work with. The front garden had been full of someone else's dream that she'd been forced to improvise around. That had its interesting aspects and challenges, too, of course. 'Using another's vision to craft your own? I've done that,' Delilah said. 'But the back? Hidden, almost? That's all mine.'

Ted only nodded. He understood the joy of growing new life, creating beauty where none had existed before, but he didn't follow what he saw as her... territoriality? But then he was awfully distracted by the way she was sitting, with her knees folded under her on the chair, leaning her elbows on the table and running a long finger down the line on the plan representing the shared driveway. One of the buttons on her shirt popped open from the strain of her position.

Then her shirt rode up her thighs and she shivered. She wasn't the only one. It seemed natural to offer her his warm bathrobe. Or maybe a blanket. His pajamas?

'You're cold,' Ted said. He stood up. She took his proffered hand. 'Come on.'

She followed him to the bedroom where his dead wife's clothes hung in the closet, but somehow, instead of Delilah adding more clothing, she had less. She did have underpants on under the pink shirt, after all. They were pink, too. Pink lace panties that matched her pink lace brassiere, and she dropped both items to make a crumpled pile on the floor with her socks. It was the last time he ever saw them, or anything of their ilk. After that first time, she always had on sensible white cotton underwear. But he didn't notice that, either.

The Streets of the Dusty Desert Town

Dolores was twelve the first time a man tried to talk her into his car. It was a sunny day in spring, not a cloud in the morning-glory sky, and many fellow middle-schoolers were both in front of and behind her as they all walked to school. No one ever walked to or from school with her.

She didn't notice the rusty truck the first time it went by – the town was full of rusted-out old trucks, what little paint was left covered with mud. Clouds of exhaust usually vied with the dust kicked up by balding tires to obscure them further. Dolores tried not to hunch into herself when the truck slowed to a creep beside her (*Show no fear, mija*, Abuela always advised during their walks), but the driver put out his grizzled head, mustache drooping over his wet lips, as he called to her. Dolores shook her head. She didn't want a ride. The truck made a horrible grinding noise as the driver slowed it down to keep pace with her.

'No, thank you,' she said when he called again. *Always be polite*, Abuela said. *Don't give passersby any excuse not to take your side.*

The truck sped up with another horrible noise, this one more like a cat with its tail caught under a rocking chair, before it pulled into the nearest driveway and the man began to descend. Dolores ran. She ran before he could cut her off from a means of escape. She ran to the group of girls half a block ahead of her, the closest protection she could see.

Miraculously, the group of girls opened and then closed around her. They sheltered Dolores in what little protection was offered by other twelve-year-old girls. Dolores saw that a taller girl – a high schooler – was among them. It was Carmen's older sister, walking her to school as older sisters were required to do. Dolores had never wanted a sister before, but she did now. The tall, kind-faced girl placed a cool hand on Dolores's shaking shoulder and left it there.

'When we get to school,' she said softly, 'I'll go with you to the principal.'

Dolores could only nod, but she wasn't sure why they had to go to the beehived lady. Despite years of trying, Dolores had never taken to the woman. She was kind too that day, but shook with anger when Carmen's sister, Rosario, told her what happened. The principal was even angrier after she phoned the police and they did... nothing. Whatever they told her, she did not repeat. She'd already sent Rosario off to the separate high school, giving her a note of excuse just in case, and she offered Dolores a carton of milk while they waited for Abuela to arrive. Dolores politely declined. She didn't need to tell the lady that her stomach was still clenched.

But she didn't see why Abuela needed to be involved, and when the tiny old lady entered, it was obvious she didn't either. Mrs Principal insisted Dolores be taken home 'to recover' and asked to be informed of the preventative steps put in place. Abuela looked at the blonde woman as if she'd spoken in tongues.

'*Claro*,' Abuela said. '*Buen día*.'

And she pulled Dolores from the room. The steps taken were these: Abuela delivered a lecture that day during their walk home. *This is the world we live in; this is what men are*. Dolores was a pretty girl; she was going to be a beautiful woman. Men were always going to be a danger until the day Dolores was old, and then she would be invisible and men would become another kind of danger... Abuela stopped talking in remembrance and Dolores shuddered with her.

Men felt entitled to Dolores's beauty and would become angry when she disagreed. Abuela said this was how they'd always been and how they'd created the world women lived in. But Dolores, and Abuela, had the right to live in it and protect themselves, and therefore from now on Dolores would wear Abuela's longest steel hatpin in the fabric of her skirt. The pin's bead head should be at thumb level, so all she had to do was slide it out, lift it up and stab.

'Aim for the cojones, *mija*,' Abuela said, demonstrating. 'Or the eye. Whatever is closest. And then pull it back out. If he isn't on his knees, do it again before you run like hell.'

Abuela rubbed her bad hip as her eyes got that faraway look. 'Run like hell and look for a woman with children or who looks like an abuela, and ask her for help.'

She abruptly stopped walking and her hand pulled Dolores to a stop before she took her granddaughter by the shoulders. Already she had to look up to meet the girl's eyes. She refused to acknowledge from whom the girl had gotten her height. Abuela squeezed her harder.

'Do not ever, never... Do you hear me? Never go to a man in a uniform for help. Not in this town. And not in any other. *Nunca, nunca, pero nunca*. Do you promise me?'

Her beautiful, wise eyes bore into Dolores's, and her sharp, strong nails cut little half-moons through the girl's blue sweater and blouse.

'I promise, Abuela,' Dolores said. She didn't cry. Her eyes were dry as the wind that buffeted them. 'I promise.'

They walked the rest of the way home in silence. Once inside, they cleaned the entire house from top to bottom. Dolores was so busy removing nonexistent spiderwebs from the ceiling with a towel-covered broom, she didn't have room to remember how her heart had raced when that man revved his truck's engine in order to cut her off, divide her from the dubious safety of other little girls. Abuela next pulled the linen from the hall cupboard and they sorted, refolded or discarded, before replacing the good linen on the freshly washed shelves. This meant Dolores couldn't imagine what would have happened if she wasn't a swift runner. She vowed to keep running, to practice at lunch on the school's tiny, badly maintained track.

When Abuela saw Dolores freeze, she dumped the rejected linens into her granddaughter's arms. Dolores stared blankly, shoulders curved around the load, as her body once more flooded in remembered panic.

'Come, *mija*,' Abuela said, and she gave the child's arm a pinch as she moved briskly into the bleach-scented kitchen. 'Let's rip these up and make them into rugs. We can sell them to Mrs Brochas – she has no home training whatsoever, poor fool. Your mama never wanted to learn how to make the rag rugs, but you are a different creature.'

Dolores was so startled at the slight criticism of her mother, sainted – or martyred, one might say – in Abuela's eyes, that she put aside her plan to become swifter, stronger, able to outrun who- ever chased her, and helped rip bed linens into pieces. She spied the steel hatpin next to a juicy blood orange, freshly plucked from their tree outside, waiting by the sink. Abuela intended her to prac- tice stabbing the fruit's plump ripeness every night until plunging the pin into resistant flesh became second nature, matter-of-fact. Dolores wasn't a squeamish girl, not by nature or nurture, and at age twelve she accepted that whenever she couldn't run away, she'd learn to stand and stab.

Fruit or man, Abuela was insistent, ultimately there was no dif- ference. Men built the world Dolores was expected to conform to, but Abuela was damned if she'd see the girl not fit to survive in it.

No one ever saw the man in the loud rusty truck again, but over the next five years there were quite a few men in town with strange limps they couldn't, or wouldn't, explain. 'They know what they've done,' Abuela would say darkly. 'And in this town, that will have to be enough.'

The Herb Garden

The day Delilah found her driveway chained and marked with that disturbing *PRIVATE PROPERTY* sign, she was thankful she'd laid claim to Ted. The chain, the sign and its message flabbergasted her. Did the sign include her? Did the chain? But it was her property, too. She possessed a deed that said so. Or Alan did, anyway. She looked forward to discussing this new development with Ted; it fell squarely in his wheelhouse, so to speak.

Delilah knew that every time she asked Ted for help, or for his opinion, or even when she accepted his small gifts and tender mercies, she broke Abuela's rules and her promise to abide by them forever. Each hour she spent with Ted, never mind if the activity was innocent gardening or something more carnal, she trampled her promises under the flimsy soles of her sneakers. Surely Abuela would make an exception? Grant a dispensation for a man as sweet-tempered and kind as Ted? Surely, the uniform didn't negate his good will – but of course, Delilah knew differently. *Fruit of the rotten tree, mija*, Abuela whispered. *Rotten.* Delilah did her best to ignore the voice and stood on the bicycle's pedals to urge the rusty old machine to a dangerous speed.

One of the reasons she preferred older men was that she felt they understood how when she asked for advice or an opinion, it was because they were mature. They'd lived longer so they knew more. Men her own generation assumed they could give advice just because they were *men*. This was the sort of stupidity that drove Delilah nuts. As her grandmother used to say: *The devil isn't wise because he's the devil, he's wise because he is so old.* Delilah never shared this *dicho* with Ted nor Alan. She doubted Ted would appreciate being compared to the devil and Alan would openly sulk at being called old.

Delilah made the long bicycle ride to Ted's side of the island in record time.

Ted wasn't home, but there was a note on the kitchen table. He didn't lock his door. No one on the island locked their doors except during mid-summer, when all the tourists ran amok, but Delilah didn't know this yet and thought Ted left his door unlocked for her, which caused her heart to swell with something like gratitude, love and pretty-girl complacency all rolled into one.

Ted had been called into an emergency budget meeting, the note read, but would call her later if she couldn't stay and wait. Delilah chuckled over the island having budget problems – the property taxes Alan paid on her behalf were extraordinary – and then started the ride home. She'd been postponing the back-garden revitalization, but tonight she'd postpone no longer. She felt the need of some bracing manual labor. That chain and its sign unsettled her.

It was still there when she arrived, daring her to do something – anything – and she entered with the same deliberation she'd used when she'd exited. She glanced irritably up at the neighboring yellow house, instigator of the sign. Per usual, it looked empty. Abandoned. No care or style devoted to making it a home in the least. Would it kill the man to put up some prettier curtains?

She put her bike in her garage and brought out a shovel, a crowbar and her wheelbarrow. Once more with tools in her hands, she felt complete. Her irritation with the man in the yellow house and his interfering sign didn't go away, but it lessened.

With tools at her fingertips, she was her most capable self; men underestimated her at their peril. Delilah adjusted the strap on her overalls, snapped the clasp in place firmly and took a deep breath. She dressed for gardening every day – except when Alan was around, of course – because she never knew when she might have to drop to her knees and pull a weed, or grab the clippers and trim back a rampaging shrub. She was prepared.

The back-garden area was paved – sort of – with large, irregularly shaped sandstone slabs. This was a travesty to Delilah, paving a garden. She'd removed the broken barbecue equipment in the dark of winter, and only a few sad willows grew at the edges of the fence line, no doubt blown in by the wind and self-seeded. Delilah intended to remove the flagstones to the front, where she wanted a path among the planted beds, and she wanted the space, here, to turn the neglected patch into an herb garden, with perhaps a small table and chairs tucked up close to the fence line for a private breakfast area. Or as private as island life could manage. But the paving had to go. She needed space to fulfill her vision.

She used the shovel to loosen the soil around the closest stone. Ted was right: the soil here was salty and sandy, and years of feet compacting it had left it hard, dry and lifeless. Delilah spent a good while digging; she didn't even think about what amendments she'd make. It wasn't time for that yet. The ground was so neglected that she had to concentrate on the labor at hand. Finally, the edges visible, she was able to drop her shovel, grab the crowbar, shove the flat end under the heavy stone and jump on the other end with her entire bodyweight.

Afterwards, she was never exactly sure what had happened. Everything was blurry but there was noise and pain. When her ears stopped ringing and her vision cleared, she found herself on the ground, in the graveled driveway. Her hand was bleeding from a gash by the thumb. The denim of her trouser leg was ripped open and her exposed shin oozed blood from shredded skin. Her tailbone blazed hellfire pain. She tried to pick gravel from the palm not bleeding, but her hand was shaking too badly, and it was only then that she realized the voice yelling, 'Are you crazy?' was not inside her head, but coming from above it.

Delilah tried to turn at the waist to face the yellow house, lost her balance from the shooting pain in her coccyx, and fell once more on her back in the gravel. From this position she saw that the window was open in the wall of the yellow house; the screen was dangling free from three corners and her neighbor's head protruded. His mouth was open. The ringing in Delilah's ears finally lessened and she could hear more than her heartbeat gushing in panicked pain. She could hear him now – he was yelling.

'Are you crazy?' He yelled it again, perhaps seeing the glazed look on her face. 'Are you trying to kill yourself? Those stones are too heavy for you! What are you thinking? Or are you thinking at all, idiot?'

His head disappeared into the house, and Delilah closed her eyes in relief. He seemed maybe ten years her senior. Not enough. Not nearly enough. And so rude.

'Here!' He was back, yelling. Delilah's eyes opened in time to see something white flutter from his hand. 'Normal people call handymen for help. This is the guy who put up the chain. Call him!'

He pulled his head back in, and she was pretty sure he called her an idiot again as he did so. He fixed the screen in place, but didn't shut the window. Delilah closed her eyes. The air smelled like strong coffee and cinnamon, and a little like her own blood.

'Hey,' his voice called again. 'Hey!'

'What!' she said, eyes still closed.

'Are you okay? Did you hit your head?'

She opened her eyes and slowly got to her feet. Limping to where the white business card lay in the gravel, she picked it up and limped back towards her side of the driveway. She was relieved he was rude and awful; he left her free not to pretend to be polite. She supposed that was a gift of a sort.

'Hey,' he called again. His voice was softer now, tentative.

'I'm fine,' she yelled up to him. 'Thanks for your concern. Thanks for the card. Now piss off.'

The neighbor laughed. Or maybe it was more of a snicker. It was immediately silenced by the slamming of the window, but she heard it. She told Ted about this interaction when she called him. He seconded the neighbor's recommendation of the handyman. Delilah would call the number after the bruises faded and the gash under her thumb was sufficiently healed. It was all too embarrassing.

It was bad enough telling Alan when he visited that weekend. Delilah was in the bathtub when he arrived and he had to search the house for her. By the time he entered the bathroom, he was annoyed; she could tell by the flaring of his patrician nostrils and the way his thin lips had disappeared altogether. He was accustomed to being greeted at the front gate by a sweet-scented, mascaraed and lipsticked girlfriend holding a gin and tonic, eager to ask about his journey and his day. It was one of her chief duties.

'Oh, hi,' Delilah said from her slouched position, and she half-waved with the hand not under the warm water in the tub. The dry hand was clumsily bandaged.

'What happened to you?' Alan walked in and looked for a place to sit. Too large for the rattan hamper and too fastidious to use the closed lid of the toilet, he settled for crossing his hands as he waited.

'Help me up?' Delilah shifted to stand. She didn't even care that water sloshed onto the bathroom floor. She hurt too much to care about housekeeping. No doubt this shocked Alan.

Alan did help her. What choice did he have, though, he and his vaunted gentlemanly identity? He took her uninjured hand as she stepped carefully over the high enamel edge onto the powder-blue bathmat. She reached for the towel over the radiator, but gasped in pain. Alan didn't cover her or help her with the towel – he was so enthralled with examining the bruises, scrapes and cuts on her body. She still stood and allowed it. *What choice do you have?* And the voice asking didn't sound like Abuela's, but her own.

'What happened to you?' There was no annoyance in his voice this time, only simple horror, and for the first time Delilah allowed herself to wonder if maybe he loved her a little. She stopped wondering with his next sentence and the blame inherent in it. 'What did you do?'

'It was a gardening mishap,' Delilah said. 'I'm worried something is broken here, though.' She put a hand to the end of her spine and turned around to show him.

Outside the open window, the curtains of Mrs Oakapple's house moved. The wind? Or a trick of the sunlight bouncing off the nearby sea? Delilah, with visions of that scary old lady staring at her that first awful day, took a quick step to jerk her new blinds closed. She then had to stand, panting for a moment, until the sharp stab in her coccyx dulled to a sickening throb and the nausea stopped.

'Yes,' she said. 'Broken.'

Alan wrapped a towel around her, finally. He was quite gentle now. 'Let's get you dressed,' he said. 'You're cold.'

'My nightgown.' Delilah pointed to the gown on its hook behind the door. It was of the type he'd normally never see on her: long-sleeved, high-necked, only saved from being raggedy by Delilah's mending skills.

'Bed?' Alan asked when she was dressed in flannel and he'd put her slippers on her feet.

'I'm hungry,' she said. Her stomach held a strange sensation, an emptiness she interpreted as hunger. 'I think. Help me downstairs?'

They discovered that after her long soak in the tub, she could only walk slowly or stand. Otherwise, she was in pain enough for tears. Delilah had thought the warm water would soothe but instead the time spent immobile had stiffened the injuries until she worried she might lose control completely and a new nature, the true self she'd never introduced to Alan, would break free. She tried to distract her mind from the panic of the pain, but cooking was beyond her, sitting impossible. She finally stretched out on the divan in the front room while Alan rummaged for a snack. He returned to sit on the rug next to her, helping her to sip tea and eat burned toast. He did this awkwardly and seemed nervous. Her nausea meant she couldn't eat after all. Delilah put her head down on a hard sofa pillow, the chintz scratching her cheek. She shut her eyes. She wanted Abuela; she had to snap out of that right now.

'You can tell me about your week,' she said. 'I'm listening.'

Alan finished his tea before clearing his throat. Delilah opened her eyes to find him studying her face. He traced a path from eyes to chin and up again; like searching for clues. When she tried to smile reassuringly – *Yes, it's me* – she failed; tears leaked and ran across her lips instead. She wanted reassurance, not to be reassuring. Alan looked out the open door where the rosemary bushes were beating against the white porch railings from the force of the wind; he didn't look at her. Perhaps seeing her in pain was his first time really seeing her. Perhaps he didn't like what he saw. Maybe she was simply light-headed from injury, and he wasn't thinking about her at all. *Not everything is about you, mija.*

'I was having lunch on Friday, in the neighborhood of our old apartment,' he said. His voice sounded tight, like he needed to clear his throat. 'Just a quick bite after a meeting and I bumped into Teresa's brother on the street. Literally bumped shoulders with Louis right on the doorstep of the old apartment.'

He paused to check her reaction. She didn't have one. She couldn't muster the energy. This was her first time learning that Louis even existed. The pain meant she didn't have to pretend to care that Teresa had a brother. Alan went back to watching the wind throw rosemary branches around outside. Delilah did love their spicy scent, released by the buffeting.

'All I could think was, what if we hadn't moved? What if we hadn't decided we needed the privacy here and you wanted more land?' Alan coughed. His voice loosened. 'It was an odd moment, seeing Louis there.'

Delilah shut her eyes once more, listening to the wind. If she concentrated, she could hear the pounding of the waves beyond the dunes, behind the wind. She didn't respond to Alan's odd moment. She had nothing to offer. She wanted someone to take care of her. She wanted someone who wanted to take care of her.

Delilah stayed on the divan that night, while Alan slept in the golden bed upstairs. In the morning, Sunday, he told her he was unsettled by the interaction with his brother-in-law on the street in front of Delilah's old apartment. She found it telling that it was no longer 'their' apartment, but only 'her' apartment. Alan felt he should return early, make sure Teresa was not suspicious. After all, Delilah was not really up for company. She asked him nicely to bring her a dress before he left. She couldn't countenance the stairs.

She was dialing Ted's number before the roar of Alan's Porsche faded down the road. Ted arrived at the cottage as Alan was driving onto the ferry. Both of Delilah's neighbors watched from their respective upstairs windows as the sheriff helped a limping Delilah into his vehicle where she reclined in the back seat, behind the safety wire. Had she had the energy, she would have found the situation funny. Or horrifying, maybe. Luckily, Abuela's voice stayed quiet.

Ted was careful not to touch her hand, which looked to be bleeding through the bandage, as he settled her, before softly closing her door and climbing into the driver's seat, making sure not to jostle her. How could anyone be afraid of him? The car backed slowly out of the driveway; the sheriff navigated the slight bump from the gravel into the paved street so gently, it was like an announcement of his love. It was a quiet day after that, filled with luminous sunlight behind cloudy skies and the gently wafting scent of bruised rosemary drifting up to lonely watchers.

Ted had been on duty when Delilah reached him. That she'd called the station when he hadn't answered at the house meant it was an emergency, and therefore he felt justified in using his patrol car to pick her up and take her to the Island Clinic. Delilah wore unlaced sneakers, a loose cotton dress and an unbuttoned cardigan that normally hung on a hook by the kitchen door. At only a shuffle-walk, tears of pain ran down her cheeks. It was really triage rules that caused the sheriff to escort her directly to the doctor.

He could ignore the judgment written on the faces of the other patients waiting. After all, he was the sheriff. This was an emergency. He would have stepped out of the exam room, he assured himself – would have waited out in his car, probably – had Delilah not clutched his elbow. Dr Papadoulos kindly averted his eyes from their clear connection, demonstrated by her ease in touching the sheriff, and unwrapped the bandages on Delilah's free hand.

'How did this happen?' The doctor's voice was kind, too. He'd been a great comfort to Ted and Gladys when she was dying.

Delilah's response was soft, nervous, jumbled. She mentioned a shovel, a paving stone and a fall in the graveled driveway. She stopped and couldn't go on. The wound under the thumb needed to be irrigated and stitched, and her coccyx was definitely broken. Delilah complied silently with the doctor's instructions and only spoke again to thank him politely before they left. Delilah in pain broke Ted's heart – she seemed even younger now. He cut off that line of thought.

In the car, Delilah wept very quietly and gave him a brief, indignant sketch of her interaction with the neighbor. Ted wasn't even tempted to laugh, and he applauded her telling the man to piss off. However, he did agree that the handyman was a safer bet than Delilah doing the heavy lifting. Delilah half-smiled, still teary-faced; she looked sheepish. Then she entered her pain-managing silence once more. Of her visit with Alan, the boyfriend, she said nothing. The man might have never existed; Ted crossed his fingers on the steering wheel.

Ted respected Delilah's silence in the back seat as he drove them to his home. He hadn't consulted her as to destination. His house had no tricky stairs, no difficult-to-maneuver graveled drive that had already bestowed injury on his girl; his house was all-round safer and easier – and he hadn't been invited into hers. He stopped thinking about that, too. Ted was becoming adept at veering from these danger areas in his mind. He'd worry about that later.

Once Delilah was safely inside and abed (she'd politely refused one of Gladys's old nightgowns), Ted sat on the edge of the bed, offering a glass of water and one of the muscle relaxants that Dr Papadoulos had prescribed for Delilah. Ted had called on his deputy to pick it up, because he wanted to get Delilah settled at home. At the back of his mind Ted realized this was as inappropriate as cutting in line at the clinic; both acts were an abuse of his station, and his home wasn't Delilah's. He pushed the thought away. Delilah's home was paid for by another man who Ted ruthlessly refused to think of for fear it would lead to other, possibly illegal, definitely abuse-of-power-type thoughts.

He brushed the silky hair out of Delilah's tear-damp eyes and set the glass of water down. He'd deal with any consequences of having Deputy Hayes doing his personal errands. Ted was the sheriff – sometimes sheriffs needed help. 'Needs must when the devil drives,' Ted said.

'Where to?' Delilah's pill was kicking in.

'Never mind,' he said, stroking her hair.

'Who is he?' Delilah said.

'The devil?' Ted smiled. She was awfully cute when she was dopey.

'No,' she said. Her teeth were gritted. She curled on her side into a pained ball, shoved Ted's pillow between her knees and pulled the covers up to her chin. 'My neighbor.'

'They say he's some kind of criminal,' Ted said softly, as if he might be overheard by the man in question. 'Mrs Oakapple and her ladies say, I mean. "Either the drugs or the guns or the Mafia with that one, Sheriff, mark my words." But no one knows – it's all just gossip.'

'What about me?' Delilah asked. Her eyes, lids swollen from tears, were closed. Her eyelashes were so long they rested on her cheeks.

Ted now stroked her arm the way his mother had stroked his when soothing him as a small, sick boy; the way Ted had stroked his dying Gladys's arm until she'd been in so much pain from the cancer eating her insides that she couldn't stand to be touched and Dr Papadoulos had visited to administer that last, large dose of morphine. But Ted refused to tell Delilah what the town's matriarchs and the town's gossips – there was overlap between the groups but they were not the same – said of her. He wouldn't speak of it and that told her all she needed to know, he saw.

She blinked slowly and carefully as he met her gaze. They were each concealing thoughts they would never willingly share. Ted would never hurt her – never, he told himself. It was more like a prayer.

Delilah's profession the islanders might not approve of, but at least they understood. Her neighbor? No one even knew his name, and his lack of occupation was downright sinister. What did he do all day, and all night, in that yellow house? Ted found his existence professionally interesting, but – aside from the neighborhood drive-bys in the cruiser – left him alone.

The islanders' tendency was towards speculation, suspicion and gossip. Actual interference was frowned upon. Delilah, her bruised ego as painful as her broken tailbone and cut thumb, appreciated the distinction. She couldn't control what people thought, but she was grateful when they controlled their actions. She'd lived with speculation her entire life; if they left it at that, left her alone, it would be the most she'd ever hoped for. She turned over in Ted's bed, closed her eyes and sought rest.

It was Ted who solved the backyard paving predicament. They were lying in bed that evening, listening to the early-summer rain falling on the elephant ears, alliums and camellia outside his bedroom window – the scent of ozone and wet Cedar of Lebanon drifting in through the partially opened window – when the idea hit him.

'Not all the flagstones,' he said, arms behind his head. 'Remove every other stone and plant the herbs in the empty spaces.'

Delilah, who had been idly finger-combing her overgrown black bangs while breathing in the sweet air, was not even momentarily confused. She carefully rearranged her legs and sat up; this was painful, but not tear-inducing. Those muscle relaxants really worked. The sheets were on the floor so she didn't bother trying to cover up. They hadn't been up to anything – Ted was too much of a natural caregiver to even expect it – but she didn't have the energy for borrowed nightgowns. Gardening was more important than nakedness.

'Eventually, the herbs will grow over the edges of the stones, too. And in the meantime, a little natural mulch will help amend the soil!' In her excitement, she grabbed one of his biceps with both hands and shook it in gratitude.

After a while they got up to consult the gardening books about herbs hardy enough to withstand foot traffic and garden furniture. They drank mint tea on the screened-in porch. Delilah wore Ted's bathrobe, even though the porch faced the backyard, with its concealing veil of old, dark pines that protected them from the collective gaze of the villagers. It was the safest Delilah had felt in... forever, she realized. Delilah felt safe with Ted. She marveled.

After a couple of days spent at Ted's house, Delilah had to clean her own. It was slow, plodding work due to her injury, but she could sense the cottage's hurt feelings over her absence and neglect, and Delilah could not – would not – live in a dusty, musty house. Cleaning was how Delilah and her home became reacquainted after Ted dropped her off in the driveway, watching her gingerly climb the porch steps and waving as she disappeared inside. Delilah didn't invite Ted into her cottage. The day he'd picked her up and driven her to the clinic was a special circumstance. It was an emergency that fell under his official purview as sheriff. It wasn't like the island had an ambulance. But inviting him into the house that Alan provided for her? That she could not do. It wouldn't be right.

Alan arrived that Friday, cross and disheveled from the journey. He didn't normally come two weekends in a row – it was suspicious, after all – but after their time together last weekend being cut short... well. He missed her; he missed their time together.

There had been a crush getting out of the city. Traffic was miserable and the Porsche was making a worrisome noise. His wife had called him that afternoon and he'd told his secretary to tell her he'd already left. The look this earned him from his secretary was also worrisome. The fact that he shared this with Delilah worried her. Was he forgetting the rules? Or changing them? She didn't care for the thought of that.

Delilah went through the motions of soothing a fractious male. She gave him a drink – today's offer was Scotch on two cubes of ice – picked up the clothes he discarded before he climbed into bed and folded them neatly over the ladder-back chair she'd refinished for this very purpose. A salad was waiting for him and she would whip up some omelets in a jiffy. She listened to his woes with sufficient sympathy but no pity, because no man wishes to be pitied, and waited until he'd completely relaxed to start telling him about her week.

But he merely seemed puzzled. He wasn't interested in her achievements: the curtains she'd sewn, the plumbing problem she'd repaired herself, the blind mole she'd accidentally caught in a gopher trap and put out of its injured misery before shoving it back into the gopher hole to show the gopher what trouble he'd caused. Delilah realized Alan was puzzled because she'd never before attempted to share her life without him *with* him.

'Maybe if I fill his house with the corpses of his friends, he'll go away,' Delilah said in conclusion, but it was obvious Alan wasn't listening. She was startled by the realization that she'd even expected him to. She was forgetting her place. *Again.* What was wrong with her?

Alan, always the gentleman, waited for her to stop talking so that he could start. Delilah, still unsettled by her mistake, obliged him.

For a moment she wondered if she were a real person to Alan at all. Did he see her as one of the porcelain dolls he bought Teresa when he traveled? When he was gone, did he think Delilah stood on a shelf in the spare bedroom, collecting dust, her black hairband box-smooth, her brown eyes painted open? The anger Delilah felt at this shocked her. She stopped wondering, stopped trying to see herself through Alan's eyes. It scared her. Violence always scared her.

To calm her mind, she began to list her changes to the cottage. She took mental before-and-after photographs, and placed imaginary captions beneath them, describing the miracles of interior decoration she'd performed. She didn't acknowledge that it wasn't Alan or even Ted to whom she addressed this internal monologue. She wasn't ready for that.

Alan carried on expounding and eating, then lounged on the bed and never noticed that Delilah was there only physically. As she went about cleaning up Alan's mess before preparing to join him in bed, her interior conversation continued.

If only he'd seen what it looked like the day she'd moved in! (Who *he* was, she wouldn't think about. He wasn't Alan, nor was he Ted. Ted didn't like to speak of the house she shared with Alan. The garden, yes. The house, no. Houses contained tables where people shared meals and beds where people shared... other things. Best not to talk about it at all.)

Alan had bought the cottage sight unseen. Of course, he'd had inspection reports and realtor photographs – he was a successful businessman after all. But the mess! And the weird piles of furniture crammed in! And the sand that had been tracked in by thirty years of renters' feet and apparently never swept back out again. *Really, people are awful*, Delilah thought. But she kept the thought to herself, as she joined Alan in bed. She turned on her side to face him, and she smiled. Or at least, she tried very hard to smile. Alan didn't even notice.

Alan supported her because she was nice to look at, easy to be around, had no interest in going public and possessed a vivid sensual nature coupled with a complete lack of inhibition. She knew this. He'd trained her, after all. And she knew what men expected of her. From her. It was drilled into her to know this, if for no other reason than her own safety.

Delilah had no ambition in life higher than growing a beautiful garden and maintaining a home of domestic comfort. Maybe Alan appreciated this as much as he did the other aspects of their relationship, the carnal ones. But he wasn't actually interested in learning how she obtained these domestic comforts. Delilah kept them to herself until Monday arrived, Alan left, and she was able to call Ted. He was such a good listener. Even if he was not exactly who she wanted to be talking to. Even if he didn't want to hear about what went on inside her cottage.

Ted couldn't help her with the labor of building the herb garden, of course. He couldn't come on the property, much less pitch in and work on Alan's territory. It wouldn't be decent. Delilah was forced to hire a handyman: the one whose card had fluttered down from her rude neighbor's window. He was the only handyman on the island, it seemed. But it was to Ted that Delilah gave a day-by-day progress report, and it was with Ted that she celebrated the herb garden's completion, drinking lemon-balm tea and eating cookies in bed. His bed. Ted's marital bed.

Of course, Delilah noticed that the progression of the herb garden's creation was watched over by the neighbor in the yellow house. She could feel him watching, a sensation as strong as the scents that wafted from his side of the driveway: browning butter and onions around lunch; the sweet vanilla tang of early-morning muffins. Yes, she saw the handyman raise a hand in acknowledgment of a former employer once or twice as he worked. If she locked eyes with the man with whom she shared a driveway when he occasionally glanced her way through his window, she never mentioned it to Ted. And she was very careful when raising her black-haired head from her tasks. She tried to avoid those accidental meetings of glances. Really, she did. She talked to her neighbor only in her head. She kept herself to herself.

The High School's
Waterlogged Lawn

The high school had nothing like a garden. It was almost exactly in the center of town. Here the desert scrub was long eradicated, and no sandstorms reached the squat stucco buildings – the only greenery around the school was the sad, soggy Bermuda grass stinking from its daily overwatering. Scraggly oleander bushes lined the limits of the property, and a few tough silk oaks planted by some forgotten school founder were much valued during lunch make-out sessions, despite their tendency to drop thick, sticky orange flowers onto the heads of the unsuspecting couples. But that was it, as far as landscaping went. There wasn't even a person hired to mow the pathetic 'lawn' – the maintenance man did it when he felt like it. Which wasn't often, because no one at the high school cared about gardening at all. The school, therefore, had nothing like a gardening club either.

It did have a Home Economics class, but after the required two years, Abuela insisted Dolores avoid the white woman – childless and never married – who taught it and ran its after-school-club component. Abuela didn't trust the bland, nuclear-orange cheese that the gringa spread on every entrée, and denigrated the method by which the woman attached sleeves to dresses. Dolores was to stay away from that woman before her good home education was corrupted completely. Dolores had enjoyed a rapport with Miss Simmons and was interested in learning more about the life of a woman who chose to stay single, but Abuela's word was law. After all, Abuela was all Dolores had left.

Dolores didn't belong to any clubs or extracurricular activities; this was the reason the guidance counselor had called her to his office. So he said. He said this while sliding all of his fingers down and up the long, fat polyester tie around his neck. Dolores stared out of his office window to where the school's concrete sign sank into the rotting lawn. Even now, the oscillating sprinklers sluggishly added to the grass's demise. Dolores didn't mourn the loss. It was long past saving.

'Without extracurricular activities,' the middle-aged guidance counselor said, 'your transcripts are pretty naked. I assume you're not planning on any further education. Gonna marry your boyfriend?'

Dolores briefly left the contemplation of the lawn to eye his left hand. The flesh bulged around the thick gold ring on his finger. His hands stopped stroking the tie for the time it took her to look, before resuming the movement once she turned away again. He petted the tie faster.

'Are you thinking about jobs, then? Your family situation...'

She caught his eye then, against her better judgment. People so rarely brought that up, and he flinched in startlement. She immediately released him, of course. It was dangerous to hold their gaze for too long, and she didn't have her hatpin handy.

She'd gotten complacent, lulled into a false sense of security. After almost four years of high school, most males had learned to keep more than an arm's distance from Dolores and her steel hatpin. The one freshman boy who tried to report her for making his thigh bleed (he had quick reflexes; she was aiming elsewhere) was beaten up after school by Carmen's boyfriend David and Carmen's twin Omero; a few other boys jumped in just for kicks.

None of these people were even friends with Dolores – she still lived a solitary life in school as in town – but snitches get stitches and the white boys needed to learn not to touch their women. Dolores may have had an Anglo *appellido*, but she lived on the brown side of town and her status was... nebulous, to say the least. Dolores understood her position, even if the boys defending her did not. But now that she was about to graduate, so close to freedom, she was accustomed to being left alone. Her hatpin was in her jewelry box. This was obviously a mistake, she realized the moment she walked into the man's office, the mustard-yellow hall pass in her hand proving her summons.

The guidance counselor ran his puffy white hand over his pomaded pompadour before he resumed stroking his tie. It clashed with his green-and-orange plaid blazer. His thin lips were wet from his constant licking of them with his fat, pale tongue. There was more than one reason it bothered Dolores to look at him.

'Most employers would be glad to have you, I'm sure,' he said. His breath hitched. Dolores's fingers clenched on the arm of the wooden chair. 'Pretty girl like you. My friend saw you at the Founder's Day picnic and asked... He has an office in need of a secretary. He'd like to help out.'

Dolores didn't look at him further, but she could no longer tolerate being in the same room as him either. She couldn't just sit there, waiting for it – him – to go further. The thought of his worm fingers touching her made her feel faint – and if she fainted, she'd be at his mercy. She couldn't handle this man, in his position of authority, with her normal small acts of violence (even if she'd had her hatpin). Her few teenaged protectors held no threat or power in this room. All Dolores could do was flee. There was only one person she could ask for help, and for the first time, Dolores thought further than her own person being threatened. *What if he does this to other girls, too, because I haven't told anyone?*

She stood up and walked out of his office, out the front doors of the high school. There was nothing in her locker she needed enough to make her pause in her escape. Afterwards, she couldn't remember the walk to her former school, or what she said to the woman at the front desk that granted her an interview with the principal – still blonde and beehived, although her body took up half the space it used to in her swivel chair and her face had collapsed in on itself. The principal now looked like an elderly Pekinese in a wig, but Dolores didn't care. She repeated verbatim what the guidance counselor had said to her and before she finished describing what his hands were doing while he talked, the principal was using her pen to dial the rotary phone. The tips of her wrinkled fingers were yellowed with nicotine.

Dolores was given gray-flecked, blue-lined paper, smelling of kindergarten and nostalgia, a pen of her own, and a little carton of cafeteria milk to pour into the cup of bitter coffee that the lady at the front desk had brought her, along with a box of tissues. Dolores didn't need the tissues; Abuela had been preparing her for this her whole life. Abuela was so beautiful in her youth that men had died for her – and she had a very low opinion of them in consequence. There was nothing they wouldn't stoop to, *mija*. *Nada*. And you never, ever, went to a man for help. Not unless you meant to invite trouble. *Un mal llama a otro.*

When the principal finished her calls, and Dolores her hot drink, the now old and obviously sick lady bundled the shaking girl (that coffee was strong) into her boat of a vehicle. The tiny old lady was forced to sit on two cushions in order to reach the pedals; this position forced her well-endowed chest into the wide steering wheel. When she turned corners, her entire upper body moved as one with the wheel. Dolores wondered how safe they were in the car, especially when the poor woman had a coughing fit and drove with one hand on the wheel and the other, handkerchief-covered, hand pressed over her mouth. The ashtray was filled with butts.

'Emphysema,' the principal said when she could gasp out words. 'Not cancer.'

'I'm sorry,' Dolores murmured politely, and she was. The principal lady was the one adult who had treated her with consistent kindness. Dolores forgave her for all those foolish tests long ago. They didn't speak again, the principal apparently not having the wind and Dolores definitely not having the inclination, until they reached Abuela's house and Dolores thanked her politely. The lady waved goodbye.

Inside the house, the shades were down, the rooms were chill and Abuela wasn't bustling around cleaning or working on her latest craft – black-thread embroidery on white altar cloth, which she intended to sell to the local Catholic church. Dolores searched the back garden – fat bees drowsing in the sun-warmed citrus blossoms were the only beings she found – before she ventured to knock at Abuela's closed bedroom door. Abuela politely, but firmly, kept that room off-limits. She had raised Dolores to respect her boundaries.

Abuela didn't answer the first tentative knock or the slightly bolder one that followed, but Dolores heard rustling within the room and took the initiative by carefully opening the flimsy old door. Abuela was resting on her bed. No, not resting. Her eyes were open, but one side of her face drooped. She was whispering out of the good side of her mouth, and her left hand was gently scratching at the chenille bedspread beneath her. Dolores dropped to her knees beside her grandmother and tipped her ear to Abuela's lips.

Aside from 'no', the words were unintelligible. Tiny bursts of air pushed against Dolores's ear. Whatever it was that she didn't want, she didn't want it with great vehemence.

'No,' Abuela whispered, her mouth sounding dry as the local wind. 'No, no, no.'

Dolores placed a shaking hand on her grandmother's clammy forehead and tried to soothe her. 'No,' she said, nodding. 'No, you're right. No, no, I agree. We won't even think about it.'

Abuela's eyes closed in exhausted relief. She moved her tongue and tried to swallow. Dolores fetched water and a spoon but Abuela only choked, waved one feeble hand and started her litany of 'no' again, so Dolores put the corner of a wet washcloth in Abuela's mouth and a slight suction was achieved. Dolores was ready to weep. What now?

With the comfort of water, Abuela lapsed back into a strange slumber as Dolores searched the room. High in the closet was a ragged photograph album that Dolores immediately confiscated and hid in her own room, and in the side table next to Abuela's bed was an address book, carefully annotated in Abuela's precise, spidery D'Nealian cursive. Here, Dolores found exactly what she needed to take proper care of the woman who had been taking care of her her entire life. Whether she wanted to or not.

Dolores never returned to the high school. Abuela required constant vigilance, and the school, informed of the guidance counselor's transgressions and castigated by the principal lady, was very happy to give Dolores family hardship leave. That summer her diploma was mailed to the tiny house surrounded by the most beautiful garden in the entire town, but by the time it arrived through the slot in the blue door, the house was empty. Abuela was buried in the town cemetery next to her daughter. Dolores left before dawn the morning after Abuela's body was removed.

Abuela's address book was filled with people and businesses two towns over, in the next state. Ever since her mother... and then her father... Abuela had said never ever go to the local townspeople for help. But plumbing goes bad beyond clogged drains, roofs develop leaks and elderly women have strokes. The doctor who came to see Abuela said there wasn't much he could do, even were they to take her to the hospital. Abuela became violently agitated at the word 'hospital' and Dolores promised her she'd be safe at home. All the doors and windows were locked. No one would even know she was ill.

The doctor left medication for pain and calmness; his nurse taught Dolores how to keep Abuela clean and comfortable. Then they got into their car and drove away, never to return until the night Abuela's breathing stilled and her fingers slowly chilled as Dolores held them to her cheek. The doctor came back, signed paperwork, and sat in the kitchen making phone calls and smoking while the nurse gave Dolores her final lesson in how to care for Abuela's corporeal needs. The pair stayed with Dolores – she was too exhausted to cry, let alone plan for the future or wonder how she was going to pay all these kind people for all their services they'd driven across state lines to provide – until the mortician arrived.

Dolores dimly recognized the old man and his middle-aged son from the day they had come to take away her mother's body. She recognized them on a visceral level, because her mind saw them through the eyes of her five-year-old self – and she walked from the room and didn't come out of the locked bathroom until the nurse softly knocked and said they'd gone.

'He's also the coroner,' the doctor said as he prepared to leave. 'I've had a quiet word. She'll be next to your mother and her wishes for no funeral will be obeyed.'

Dolores only nodded, shook the doctor's hand and allowed the nurse to embrace her, before she locked the door behind them to begin clearing out any storage areas in Abuela's room and collecting a tidy pile of items pertaining to her mother that she'd never seen before. There was a cedar box with newspaper clippings, a baby album with her mother's black baby curls and a glued-in envelope containing milk teeth brittle with age. She found birth certificates, a marriage license and a death certificate. She didn't find any jewelry, nor did she expect to, knowing Abuela had sold anything and everything, including her worn wedding band, in order to pay the bills incurred by raising a grandchild in a town in which no one would employ her, even before she was too old to employ. No one wanted the living reminders of the murdered woman around, neither the mother nor the child – reminders of the town's collective guilt.

Dolores dumped out a box holding a large, veiled hat that Abuela must have bought sixty years ago, when feeling ostentatious, and placed the family treasure she'd unearthed inside. This box fit neatly in half of the one suitcase Dolores allowed herself, which meant most of her clothing had to be left behind. Not that she had an extensive wardrobe.

Dolores put on layers of proper traveling clothes and her good school shoes, turned off all the lights, picked up the single, heavy suitcase, and walked out the door she locked behind her. She dropped the keys back inside the mail slot. She didn't know to whom the rent was paid, and she didn't care. The sun was lightening the horizon when she arrived at the bus stop on the outskirts of town, the last star disappearing as she stepped on board and paid the driver from the tiny supply of cash in the black, pillbox pocketbook she'd taken from Abuela's closet – unwrapped from its nest of tissue paper – because she thought it was pretty. The bus doors closed with a screech of finality and Dolores never looked back through the cloud of dust as the bus took her away from the only home she'd ever known. Without Abuela, it wasn't home, wasn't safe. The first gift Dolores could give her grandmother was leaving.

Later on, when Dolores's diploma fell through the mail slot in the blue door, onto the carpet with all the other circulars and bills in the musty darkness of the empty house, Abuela was already buried. The coroner had kept his word; Abuela was buried and the child gone, the house empty, before the townspeople even knew Abuela was dead. The kindly beehived principal was considered the last person to have seen Dolores after she waved a polite goodbye that day. Or, at least, the principal was the only one who would admit to seeing her; the others were all paid by the kindly doctor from out of state for their discretion. Dolores didn't know how to pay any of them for their services or kindness, so she skipped town instead. If they were friends of Abuela's in any capacity, she was sure they'd understand.

Dolores never knew how Abuela had met her network of helpers or how much help they'd indeed given, or what was said behind closed doors or to whom. We none of us will ever know.

The Yellow House

Anton was in exile. Anton was in exile on a small, lonely island in a large, drafty house with terrible lighting. Anton couldn't stop thinking of Napoleon lately. 'Able was I ere I saw Elba.' But this island wasn't Elba and Anton wasn't Napoleon. He had to stop thinking like that.

Anton wasn't Napoleon; he didn't want to conquer the world. Anton wasn't even John Dillinger. He hadn't killed anybody or extorted money from anybody, or driven anybody around who had either murdered or extorted money. Anton had merely worked in a restaurant where people who murdered or extorted money liked to eat, and one night a few years ago Anton had witnessed something that many people, including Anton, would have preferred he not witness.

One of the groups of people who didn't fall into this category, the FBI agents trying to build a RICO case against the restaurant's patrons, persuaded Anton (who hadn't always been named Anton) that it was in his best interest to turn state's evidence, and then disappear. Which is why Anton was exiled to this island, a protagonist in a story no one would believe were Anton able to tell it to them. He was trying to write that story. He was writing a book.

It was pointless to write the book, Anton knew, because his keepers would never allow him to publish it. It was pointless to write the book, but he was doing so anyway. Mostly he was writing the book because the island where Anton was exiled had nothing like a restaurant. There was a small coffee shop, an ice-cream shoppe, a candy store open only in the summer for the tourists' kids and the drugstore counter that sold sandwiches; but there wasn't what Anton would call a restaurant. Islanders went to the mainland for any 'fancy' dining.

Anton often thought about opening one. During his first lonely days of exile, he'd dragged himself out of his damp bedroom with plans of setting up a true Italian grotto of a restaurant. Anton planned the full stereotype for the islanders. Red-flocked wallpaper, black-and-white tiled floors, gold-painted chairs or black velvet-lined booths – maybe some of each. Every table would have a netted wine-bottle candleholder and the waitresses would wear loosely tied peasant blouses with full-tiered skirts. Preferably, Anton would have them all barefoot and languid to the point of rude, but he knew it didn't matter. He knew all his plans were for nothing.

The plans grew more elaborately strange and implausible as his first winter gloamed on, because he knew these plans would never come to fruition. A restaurant would be the first place the murdering extorters would look for him. A restaurant was Anton's natural setting. Lions lived on the veldt, sharks swam in the sea and Anton belonged in a dim, smoky restaurant. Therefore, he was writing a book. It had a lot of recipes, his book, but it wasn't a cookbook. He called it a memoir. A memoir that talked about food. A lot.

'Anyone who thinks seven recipes for lasagna is too many,' he'd mutter to the photograph of his dead nonna propped next to his typewriter, 'is someone who doesn't understand the importance of sauce.'

She didn't speak back, of course. At least, not yet. By the second year, Anton was beginning to worry that eventually she might. Or a nod or wink of agreement would appear in evidence. Anton worried that while he was waiting around to testify, he was also waiting to lose his mind. Writing the cookbook – the memoir – helped to avoid this; cooking helped, too. But mostly he was just waiting.

In the meantime, Anton ran. Sometimes he ran twice a day if the words didn't come. Sometimes there were problems with the house – the drafty, dark, ugly yellow house (Elba) – and Anton would call one of the approved numbers taped next to the phone in the kitchen. He was embarrassed to admit how much he looked forward to these few-and-far-between interactions and how sometimes he thought about sabotaging his own home in order to instigate another call. Because, otherwise, Anton only saw people, talked to people, when he drove to the mainland – the ancient Renault riding the ferry like a child's bathtub toy – to shop for groceries and check in with his assigned marshal. Anton loved grocery shopping. He loved squeezing the melons at the greengrocer's, sampling the cheeses at the dairy, discussing the choicest cut of meat with the butcher, who admitted to enjoying arguing with this customer who knew a little more about food than was normal for local men. Grocery shopping was the best part of Anton's month. He hated meeting his marshal.

He couldn't help but admit that her air of slight disappointment in him hurt his feelings. She even looked a bit like a younger version of his nonna. But it didn't matter: as she was the only woman in his life, and one with great authority, he lived in fear of losing her esteem. She was the only person who knew where, and who, he was. She was his last connection to reality. Whenever he remembered this, Anton needed to go caramelize an onion to calm his nerves.

Anton had been in exile for almost two years when the girl moved in next door. The cottage was on the market. The marshal seemed irritated by this fact when Anton moved in, but not worried. The little house was overpriced and too inconvenient to be a quick sale, the marshal said. Look at that ridiculous driveway. The cottage had been a rental before Anton's time, but while for sale, it sat empty and forlorn. He had the posts and chain installed at the mouth of the driveway his first summer because the tourists parking under his office window made him nervous, and the cars blocking access to his garage – and therefore his trip to the mainland – enraged him. The marshal agreed that so many people bumbling around the property was a recipe for disaster. The marshal laughed at the pun. Anton did not. Neither tourists nor recipes were laughing matters to him.

Anton called the marshal-approved handyman, had the posts and chain added, and forgot about the empty cottage. Until the day the black-haired girl moved in. Her bustle and cleaning, the lights at night shining into the driveway, the sounds of a chainsaw *inside the house*, were impossible to ignore – and once seen, she was impossible to forget. He stopped thinking about Napoleon that day and started feeling like a character closer to Rapunzel. He liked that feeling even less. The morning she called herself Cinderella in that dark, smoky voice, like she'd been reading his mind, he almost fainted. Luckily, she made it very clear that she had no intention of rescuing him, when she backed away into the gloom of her garage to avoid speaking to him, and she made sure never to interact with him again. *Yes, luckily*, Anton reminded himself. He was fortunate that she was completely uninterested in him. Her avoiding him was a good thing.

The black-haired girl was also a runner. Anton would pass her occasionally, his eyes meeting hers against his will. She was beautiful, sexy, a little goofy, but not remotely friendly. He again reminded himself this was for the best. His next-door neighbor, this person who mysteriously appeared as if from nowhere, with her chainsaw, was not someone he should get involved with.

'Don't shit where you eat,' Nonna would have advised him. So he didn't. But it was advisable to keep an eye on her. After all, what did he know about the intriguing dark beauty next door? She could be a mob assassin. It was unlikely, given that she only cleaned and gardened and rode the rusty bicycle she'd found in her garage that first day he heard her voice. Aside from that, she didn't even know that he, Anton, was alive, let alone seem interested in killing him. It was enough to hurt his feelings.

But one morning during his run, he swerved to avoid driftwood and she was forced to acknowledge his existence. Her head jerked at his movement in her peripheral vision and she swung around to meet him face to face. She caught his eyes with her own, big and dark. He swerved again in immediate, tingly reaction. After that, when they met, there was maybe a head nod of greeting. Later on, Anton glimpsed a smile on her face when he sneezed so hard, he broke stride and the waves splashed his shoes. She would find that funny, he supposed. She really was quite goofy. And gorgeous, damn. When she smiled, he missed another step.

Even sweaty, no make-up, her hair tied in a sloppy ponytail with one of those thick rubber bands that held broccoli stems together, when she smiled she was so beautiful that Anton was tempted to break the rules and stop running. He wanted to speak to her. He wanted to know her name. He wanted to hear her voice again. He stopped this line of thinking and headed home.

However lonely in his exile, Anton knew better than to start something he couldn't finish. Nevertheless, he made sure he never mentioned his new neighbor's existence to his marshal during his monthly visit. The marshal would have questions, and questions would lead to investigations, and possibly that could lead to Anton moving or somehow losing sight of his beautiful, black-haired neighbor. As much as Anton hated Elba, now that he'd found his Josephine he didn't want to leave.

Anton heard the screen door slam one Saturday morning. Normally, she was quiet in her movements, now that she'd finished destroying the furniture. She made no noise unless the man was around. Anton stepped to the window to look down into the back garden. Her arms were full – that's why the door had slammed shut behind her. She held two brown paper bags – one spilling ears of corn, one empty – and a large saucepan.

'You overbought,' Anton muttered. No two people could eat that much corn, and most people didn't cook it properly anyway.

She sat on the lowest step, gingerly, her bare feet in the grass below and her legs, exposed by the short dress, in danger of splinters from the aged wooden steps. She was most likely uncomfortable, the day not quite warm enough for her outfit, because she frowned as she began shucking the corn, dropping the naked ears into the tall stockpot.

'No, no, no,' Anton whispered. She was going to boil it. This was just bad. Anton would peel the husks down, but not off. He'd remove the silk carefully, then rub the exposed kernels with butter and seasoning, before rewrapping the corn in the husks and roasting it over tired coals.

The black-haired girl was placing the husks and silk in the empty paper bag. She performed this job neatly, gracefully, but with none of the joy she exhibited when gardening. Even when burying dead rodents, she'd looked more gleeful than she did now, shucking corn.

'Delilah!' A voice yelled from inside the cottage. Anton leaped away from the window, only to leap back almost immediately. Yes, like a rabbit. The last two years had turned him into a rabbit; he could admit that to himself. But on the porch across from him, the girl was startled, too. No one could compare Delilah to a rabbit. She dropped the corn she was holding. It bounced down the steps to land in the patchy grass.

'Delilah, where are my shoes?'

Anton knew it was the boyfriend. He knew the guy existed, was there that weekend, of course. Hence the absurd amount of corn. Delilah would never be that wasteful. Anton didn't like the boyfriend: witness the idiot's inability to find his own shoes. Anton preferred to pretend the guy didn't exist. This was difficult when he kept yelling.

'Delilah!'

'Find your own damn shoes,' Anton said.

As if she had heard this, Delilah looked up at his window, where he stood watching her. Shocked by the connection of their gaze, he froze. With their eyes locked, he read the thoughts written on her face. She was also thinking, *Find your own damn shoes*. Anton knew it, sure as he knew his name. Well, no. The name was not his. He knew what Delilah was thinking sure as he remembered the yeasty smell of his nonna's baking focaccia. He and Delilah had been staring into each other's eyes for so long now that Anton was uncomfortable. Wasn't he? At least, he should be.

He dropped the curtain and stepped back. That was creepy. No doubt she thought so, too. Anton had moved a cot into his office. Not exactly because it overlooked the shared driveway; this side of the house was warmer, drier. His bedroom and living room were on the damp, dark side of the yellow house. The kitchen was on the warm, dry side. He practically lived in the kitchen, anyway. The kitchen led to the deck where he ate breakfast when it was sunny, drank wine when it was dusk, and sat to put on or take off his running shoes. Anton had more enthusiasm for living now that Delilah was next door. But he had no intention of talking to her.

All his best intentions flew out the window he opened in order to yell at her the day he watched her almost brain herself with a crowbar. It was the same day he'd put up the driveway chain for the season. Tourists were beginning to arrive on the island by way of the ferry and Anton had that morning, before his run, clipped the chain with its sign to the concrete posts. After his run, he'd taken his breakfast – blueberry and flaxseed muffins he'd baked earlier – to the office overlooking the driveway. He kept a comfortable chair far enough from the window so as to rest his feet on the sill, and be able to look out and yet not be seen. Anton's book lay abandoned on the desk, next to his typewriter. Both were dusty.

Anton watched Delilah fetch her bike, discover the chain and read the sign before riding away. The intense stink-eye she cast his house after reading the sign was not in his imagination. He smiled in satisfaction. He'd made her cranky; Delilah couldn't pretend he didn't exist if he irritated her. Good to know.

Lately when she left on her rides, she'd be gone for hours, so Anton went downstairs to clean the kitchen and do some laundry. When he heard the chain rattle, signaling Delilah's return, he peered out the kitchen window in time to see her disappear into the garage. She emerged with garden implements and Anton raced back to his viewing chair.

She was digging around one of the large stones that paved the backyard. That was weird, but then she was the same girl who had chopped down her laundry line for a bonfire. When she dropped the shovel and picked up the crowbar, jamming the flat edge under the stone, Anton found himself on his feet. His cup of coffee hit the floor. He made it to the window just as, down below, Delilah threw all her weight on the crowbar. Anton didn't have time to open the window before the stone's greater weight countered Delilah's and she was flung backwards. The stone scraped down her leg as it landed back in its place; the crowbar jerked from her grasp. Her slight form hit the gravel, butt-first, and slid.

Anton left his body. The window was open, the screen loose, and he was yelling while hanging half-out of the yellow house before he was able to stop the body he was no longer controlling. Delilah wasn't answering him. Oh God, was she dead? Wait, no. She was moving. She was answering. She sounded embarrassed, annoyed, in pain. Her voice was huskier than he thought it should be. Was she trying not to cry? She was bleeding; she was shaking. Anton needed to go down and help her.

No, he didn't. He needed to stay far away. But damn, she needed *someone* to help her. Someone needed to protect her from her enthusiasm, her hubris. There was such a thing as too much confidence, he wanted to tell her. Thinking you're invincible was dangerous, he knew.

Anton pulled his head inside, fetched the handyman's card from his desk and threw it to the girl in the driveway. There, he'd done what he could. And now Delilah sounded angry. Did she just tell him to piss off? Anton was laughing at a beautiful woman telling him to piss off; this was dangerous. He'd always liked them a little mean. He went to the kitchen and brewed a fresh pot of coffee. Drinking it, he found himself back in his body. Back in Elba.

He avoided the window all weekend once he saw the sheriff pick her up, and he didn't see Delilah when he was out running. He doubted she would be capable of running for a while, with the state of her shinbone and what looked like a broken ass. The boyfriend had showed up (speaking of asses) and then left again right away. No-good bastard. Anton didn't understand what Delilah saw in that guy.

Monday morning, Anton found a paper bag of freshly cut Swiss chard on the floor of his deck. It looked like she'd shoved it between the rails. She must have held it over her head and stood on her tiptoes to reach. That would have hurt. She'd given herself pain to give him a gift. This knowledge did something to Anton's insides. They felt warm and runny, like an improperly baked lava cake. Or how he preferred to eat his eggs. He shouldn't accept the gift. He wasn't supposed to fraternize or familiarize, or something, with the natives, the marshal said. But fresh Swiss chard! Anton could make a pesto to die for with Swiss chard.

He put the bag in the refrigerator and went for his run. Afterwards, he showered and shaved and got spiffed up, looking forward to a day out. Then, when opening the garage to get his car out for the monthly mainland trip, he was made to pay for the gift.

'Hi,' Delilah said.

Anton turned, startled. He had no idea how she'd snuck up on him in the graveled driveway, but then saw she was on her grass verge and she was barefoot. Her hands, as well as her knees exposed by cut-off jeans, were muddy. She'd been weeding. Hidden by the monstrous plants in her front garden, using his joy at a day out as a distraction, she'd struck. She was a cobra, beautiful and stealthy.

'Hi,' she said again. 'I left you some greens—'

'Yeah, thanks. I found them.' Anton forced himself to speak so she would stop. Her husky voice slayed him. He was pleased he had remembered the tone correctly. He wasn't completely mad yet.

'I called that handyman,' she said, brushing the drying dirt off her hands. 'He's coming out soon.'

Anton didn't know how to respond, so he finished opening the garage door. He worried that he was staring at her. After two years, he didn't know how to talk to people in general, let alone beautiful women with whiskey voices, anymore. He removed the chain from the left-hand post of the driveway, eyeing her from the side of his vision.

'About that chain,' Delilah said.

Anton stopped and turned. She stopped talking, looked him in the eyes and put her hands in her pockets. One hand was still bandaged. Her shin injury was scabbed over. The pause was lasting too long, the eye contact as well. Anton couldn't move away. He didn't want to.

'Is it really necessary?' she finished asking with a shrug.

'Yes,' he said. 'It is.'

She sighed. He sighed in response. He couldn't stop the sigh and that irritated him. He was a grown man. He'd owned a restaurant; he'd had a life. Delilah's head tilted; she noticed him now. Or was it his mood?

'Look,' he said, and she laughed.

He gripped the driveway chain tightly (her laughter killed him) and started over.

'You've never seen what these tourists are like in the height of summer. They're like locusts. They're everywhere. They block the driveway, block the garage, drop trash. They are awful.'

Delilah started to smile. He hurried to stop the smile, her devastating smile, from forming. A glimpse of her one crooked eyetooth would be his downfall. Delilah smiling at him was even more dangerous than Delilah giving him the stink-eye. *But either way, she's looking at me*, he couldn't help thinking.

'They drop trash *everywhere*,' he said. He spoke sternly to disguise his melting insides. 'What if they got in your garden, huh? How would you like people stomping through the vegetables, dropping trash?'

She stopped smiling and her eyes widened. She glanced over her shoulder into her garden, anxious now. The squash vines were climbing up the corn stalks, the giant sunflowers were not yet giant but showed promise, and the marigolds edging the beds were riotous bangs of color as they bloomed their red-gold and orange heads off. 'Okay,' she said. 'The chain stays.'

Anton nodded and dropped the end of the chain that he'd been holding tightly. She stepped forward, into the gravel, closer to him. Her bare feet on the uneven ground made her wobbly. He should *not* hold her elbow to steady her. He stepped back.

'My name's Delilah,' she said. 'What's yours?'

Anton felt light-headed. He took a few more steps towards the safety of his car. The unpaved garage smelled like gasoline, mildew and loneliness. She was waiting for his answer.

'My name is Anton.'

'Really?' She narrowed her eyes and tilted her head again, like she saw right through his lies.

'No,' he said, and immediately thought, *Oh my God.*

'Really?!'

'Do you even have a sense of humor?' He sounded like a jerk, but she was laughing.

'Go on,' she said, waving him to his car. She picked up the chain from the gravel. 'I'll close it behind you.'

Anton fled. He got in the car that wasn't his, drove it to the ferry, crossed the water and met with the marshal who, unfortunately, was his. He was out of his body again. Anton was not accustomed to the sensation. Maybe he never would be, but he was beginning to enjoy it. For the first time in his two years and four months of exile, Anton couldn't wait to get back to Elba. He'd worry about that later.

To the Sea

Abuela's address book led Dolores to her grandmother's cousin Gisela. The town where Gisela lived was two days away – two days on the bus after the dawn escape. Dolores stepped from the bus into a town, not dusty but otherwise indistinguishable from the town in which she had grown up. She was so weary, she could barely take in her surroundings, and a strange haze hovered in the periphery of her vision. Whether it was her eyes or the weather, she neither knew nor cared.

It was late afternoon when she called Gisela's number from a telephone in the mechanic's shop that doubled as the bus stop. The mechanic gave Dolores the use of his own phone when her coin purse proved empty. She was so tired and hungry that she started to shake when she realized she would have to ask for change. She hadn't felt safe leaving the bus when it stopped for food and was too anxious to do more than occasionally drop off, her head bouncing against the headrest of the window seat she'd claimed that early morning when the bus was only three-quarters full. Her hand shook so hard as she dialed Gisela's number that the mechanic took the receiver from her and dialed Gisela himself, from memory. Dolores hadn't known if the number was still correct; what if Abuela's cousin had moved or died?

'*No te precupes, mija*,' the large mechanic said as he handed her the phone. '*Aquí lo tienes.*'

Gisela was alive and seemed overjoyed to hear from Dolores, even while she cried a little at the news of her favorite cousin's death. Cousin Gisela immediately invited her to stay in her home, vacant these many years of children and only occasionally visited by grandchildren. 'Not that I blame them – they all have such busy lives. My children have done well, I am happy to say.' There was a pause, as she no doubt thought of her cousin's daughter, Dolores's mother.

'I won't give you directions, sweetheart,' Gisela said, breathlessly. 'It's too far to walk. Hand the telephone to Mr Melendez and I'll have him drive you over.'

The mechanic's teenage son was enlisted to drive Dolores across town to her cousin. The boy straightened from his bored lounging in the dirty, crammed office that smelled of grease and gasoline when he saw Dolores's drooping, bus-rumpled person. He was so intimidated by her creased beauty that after giving her a bottle of soda and a candy bar, and carrying her suitcase, he only spoke again when she politely thanked him for the ride and he choked out an incongruous, 'Yes, ma'am.' He then blushed brighter red than the borrowed car.

Dolores, heady with the knowledge that this boy close to her age was oblivious to her background and story, tipped her head at her suitcase in the back seat and raised her eyebrows until he remembered to carry the too-heavy-with-history luggage to the door for her. He then loped back to the car to wait for the house's door to open and tiny Cousin Gisela to welcome the girl in. Days later, by the time the mechanic's son had worked up the nerve to stop by and see if Dolores was interested in another drive in another borrowed car, or perhaps a film, she was gone. He couldn't shake his disappointment, even though the answer would have been 'no', as not only his father, but Gisela, too, told him. Dolores's life plans didn't include sixteen-year-old boys reading comic books, but she did appreciate the candy bar. Dolores had a sweet tooth.

She slept for twelve hours after Gisela put her to bed in the tiny guest room, a pink coverlet smelling of lavender tucked under her chin. Gisela asked questions as she readied the room, which the sad girl politely answered. They were mostly questions about her life with Abuela, and the old woman's illness and death. Gisela didn't dare go further back than that yet. Otherwise, Dolores didn't offer much information, poor tired thing.

By the next day, all caught up with sleep and missed meals, Dolores realized that she couldn't stay in this small town either. Gisela was closely related enough not to need to ask about the death of her mother or the disappearance of her father, but Dolores could see her thinking about it. Dolores had never lived with people who weren't thinking about it every time they looked at her. She could only dream about people who saw her not as the child of a murder victim and a murderer, but simply as Dolores. She was never just a pretty girl. She wondered what that would feel like.

'I told Lola, your abuela, to move here,' Gisela said over breakfast. She was mending an old sweater, previously owned by her married daughter, for Dolores to wear in the cool evenings. 'I told her we had family here, enough to protect both of you. You didn't need to be so alone.'

Gisela reached out to pat her hand, frozen in the act of buttering toast. She missed because the girl dropped both the toast and the knife, and used both hands to grip the edge of the table. Gisela thought to reassure her, the way she would a child of her own.

'Lola didn't have to raise you in fear.' Gisela spoke to Dolores only in English, not knowing if Lola had ever taught her granddaughter their mother tongue. The gringo-father had not allowed it in his house – this, Gisela knew.

'She didn't raise me in fear,' Dolores said quietly, staring at the dropped toast on her plate. 'She wasn't afraid. She was waiting. She didn't leave, in case he came back.'

Then Dolores stood and walked to the bedroom, leaving half her breakfast uneaten. Gisela finished it – no waste in her house – while she sat and digested what she'd learned. Lola was always bold, confident in her great beauty and sharp intelligence, and everyone knew that Graciela, her baby, *su querida*, was the love of her life. And *pequeña* Dolores was the love of Graciela's. Otherwise, Lola would have died to protect her daughter that night instead of living to raise the grandchild. This, Gisela had known from the beginning, but staying in that town? That town of collective murderers; those people who knew exactly what was happening in that house and not only did nothing to stop it, but they helped the murderer escape when he finally finished what he'd started with his fists. Choosing to live surrounded by those people? That, Gisela had never understood. Lola would never speak of it – not on the telephone in whispered conversations when the child slept, nor in the letters she and Gisela exchanged as Dolores grew older and Lola took care to avoid speaking of her mother's death in front of her. Lola was never one who deigned to explain her actions.

Gisela understood now, with her own mother's heart. Lola spent the last part of her life waiting for her daughter's killer to return and preparing for revenge. Raising Graciela's child to survive and escape was part of that, of course. Maybe it would have been better for young Dolores if they had left, but she understood why Lola had not. Gisela neatly folded the mended sweater belonging to her daughter, living across town with her own small family. She thought of what she would do were anyone to hurt Natalia; then she nodded in approval of Lola's actions, before getting up to clean the kitchen.

*

When Dolores emerged from the guest room, bathed and dressed, looking eminently wholesome in her proper cotton dress and thin linen coat, Gisela caught her breath at the resemblance to Lola, the child's grandmother, at the same age. She wanted to embrace her, but Dolores twitched in surprise so Gisela changed her movement and handed the girl the perfectly mended mohair sweater.

'*Gracias, prima*,' Dolores said and she folded the item neatly over her arm. She looked flustered, slightly regretful that she'd missed the hug. 'Where would I find a typewriter?'

Gisela directed her to the local library, even drew her a little map, all the while realizing that although she was the image of her grandmother – the image! – inside, she was not the same. Lola had been fire; look at her plan to seek justice for her child. This girl, Dolores, smooth and calm, was ice. If she took revenge in hand, Gisela thought as she watched the girl walk down the sidewalk and through the creaking gate, little Dolores wouldn't wait patiently, burning. This Dolores (Gisela had never met anyone less likely to be nicknamed 'Lola') would boldly make her plans and then hunt her father down. Gisela thought that Anglo policeman was lucky his daughter had no interest in vengeance. Very lucky indeed.

Gisela had accepted a girl named Dolores Ortiz without question; naturally the girl would be named for her grandmother, Dolores mused during her walk. Dropping her Anglo father's last name when she introduced herself at the mechanic's bus stop was Dolores's first move towards independence and anonymity. Abuela's birth certificate was old, brittle, sepia-colored; Dolores was easily able to erase the birth date. She did this in the open, at the library that smelled of air conditioning, leaded ink and respectability. No one even looked at the task she was engaged in, not when they could study her grace, her long black hair pulled back from the heart-shaped face to spill down her shoulders, covering the blue cotton of her modest dress. No one knew *who* she was here; they only cared what she looked like. Dolores wanted more of this anonymity, this power in being mysterious.

Be brazen, Abuela always said. *Be confident. No one will question the right of a beautiful woman to do want she wants, as long as she does it in the open, where they can watch her. Where they think they own her with their eyes.*

Sitting at the typewriter, in the cool dusty room filled with the smell of old books, crumbling leather bindings, and the open newspapers several men and women were pretending to read, Dolores saw that the first name on the birth certificate was mostly rubbed away. It hardly stated Dolores at all. There was a strong capital D and a legible lowercase L, but as for the rest, it was mostly guesswork. The girl known until then as Dolores drummed her fingers on the wooden table – one two three four, one two three four – as she thought about Abuela's favorite Bible story. Then she put her fingers on the typewriter keys and corrected the illegible name on the birth certificate. She added her own date of birth in the proper space.

She breathed a sigh of relief – almost pleasurable, the roots of her hair tingling – and then Delilah Ortiz got up and walked out of the library. That the expectations of others and their too-common disappointments didn't visibly fall from her to land like broken glass bubbles behind her footsteps was an honest surprise. Delilah felt their weight leaving her shoulders and she heard them shiver into pieces upon the shiny tile floor. Her liberated smile was fierce, but not directed at anyone other than her own secret self. She made sure of that.

Delilah and her smile were never seen in the library again, much to the disappointment of the many patrons and staff who had watched her that day, although the clerk in charge of the typewriters expressed dismay that when the beautiful girl had left, she'd taken the typewriter's brand-new ribbon with her. No one listened to his ramblings about what she might be hiding, of course; that lovely girl could not be capable of anything underhanded. With beauty like that, nothing she could do would be bad.

Within a few days, Gisela put her sweet-tempered cousin on a bus – with her failing eyesight she couldn't catch the destination – with newly mended but nice enough cast-offs in her suitcase and a small carpet bag that Natalia was happy to donate to the cause. Quiet Dolores made no remarks as to where she intended to go or what she would do once she got there, and by now Gisela had learned not to ask. The guilt she felt at not doing more for Lola after her tragedy, she offset by doing what little Dolores would allow her to do now. She was allowed to feed her, clothe her, give her a room and a little traveling money – all the while keeping her mouth shut about the past. This was hard for Gisela, genuine work, and she was quite relieved as the beautiful girl got on the bus and left their lives. But she would never admit that. Never.

She did what she did for love, she told Natalia. Love, and family loyalty. But she knew the truth in her heart, and she thought maybe Dolores did, too, for although Gisela received a thank-you note and some postcards from Dolores, which continued to arrive until the day Gisela passed and all her secret heartaches were over, the notes were without return address and all were signed with nothing more than a large, florid D.

Delilah got off the eastbound bus when the air smelled of wet salt and her elderly seatmate mentioned a famous botanical garden in the city proper. *Always choose a grandmother type to sit next to on the bus* was the advice Delilah would give her own daughter in the future. Delilah learned this lesson during the three days she traveled the country, moving from seat to seat as she was made uncomfortable, awkward or just plain threatened. That last one involved a smelly man in a dirty coat who whispered things she barely understood and would never repeat to her daughter or *anyone* for that matter; she stood and walked away, up front.

Her refusal to repeat what the horrible man had said made it difficult when she tried to report the interaction to the bus driver. He, another smelly, creepy man busy shoving pork cracklings into his mouth with the hand not on the large steering wheel, did nothing but shrug (*What did you expect?* Abuela sniffed in Delilah's head). That was when the elderly lady reached out from her seat behind the driver, took Delilah's hand and pulled her into the empty seat next to her, shoving aside a handbag, lunch box, a shawl and an industrial-sized Thermos to make room for her.

The lady was wearing a Sunday-best traveling suit, complete with a tiny hat bearing wilted velvet violets, and she smelled like baby powder and respectability. Delilah didn't want to let go of her gloved hand. This nice lady – if she said her name, Delilah didn't catch it – gave her a starched hanky to wipe her eyes (the words she'd received from that man had felt like blows, even if she didn't understand exactly what he was implying – his intent was violent and clear) and sips of weak instant coffee from the tiny traveling cup attached to the Thermos, all while patting Delilah's trembling shoulder. She was so much like a kinder, homely, less cosmetically enhanced Abuela that the emotionally bruised Delilah was tempted to follow her home and see if she needed an adopted granddaughter. But the Violet Lady was headed to her son's house to move in and help her daughter-in-law through a dangerous pregnancy.

'Her last baby was huge and breech – that means feet-first, dear – and Ethel could only walk backwards for two weeks after the birth,' Violet Lady said, and Delilah decided to never have sexual intercourse ever. 'It was recommended that the sweet girl not have another, but men being what they are... Well, I'm a little upset with my son, so it seems the least I can do is go and help. And maybe put a little saltpeter in Matthew's meals.' She chuckled, so Delilah smiled politely, though she suspected her seatmate had just admitted to planning to poison her son.

Violet Lady opened a tin of tiny cookies, strange unnatural colors, but a hungry Delilah murmured a polite thank-you and ate them neatly, as Violet Lady's story went on.

'Had I time, dear,' – the Violet Lady patted Delilah's non-cookie-holding hand – 'I'd get off this bus soon and spend a day at the garden. Famous it is, but I can't remember the name. Do you like gardens, dear?'

Delilah, mouth full, nodded enthusiastically. Well, as enthusiastically as one could with one hand holding cookies and the other a tiny cup of weak coffee, and in the knowledge that a perverted predator lurked nearby. But she didn't like gardens; she loved gardening. There was a difference. If her mouth hadn't been full, she'd have tried to explain. The Violet Lady didn't seem to need an explanation, though.

'It's not too far now, the town with the garden, and there's lots of signage leading you to it. You can't miss it.' Then, coffee gone and cookie tin depleted, she rested her head on Delilah's shoulder and went to sleep.

Violet Lady woke when the bus stopped for gas and to allow the passengers to use the facilities. She pointed out that they'd reached the town with the garden and wished Delilah good luck before going back to sleep. Delilah's empty seat she filled once again with her accoutrements, until the next besieged woman needed it. Delilah admired her ingenuity as she pointedly ignored the bus driver, disembarked and proceeded deeper into town, walking on bus-wobbly legs under the weight of her past-laden suitcase.

Delilah was quite tired, and a little worried, when she finally found the garden and inquired of a man in overalls outside the gates, busy digging a drainage culvert clear of kudzu, where she'd find the employment office. He grunted disinterestedly until he looked up and she smiled her crooked eyetooth smile. Digging clay soil was taxing, thankless labor, she knew. And her full smile was irresistible – she'd known that since junior high school. The man put down the spade, brushed off his hands and climbed out of the ditch. He was so tall Delilah had to tip her head back to look him in the eye. His face was stern.

This serious man did not know her. He knew nothing about her, aside from the pretty blank slate of her face. Delilah was free to be whoever he needed to see, whoever could get what she wanted from him. His face was stern, yes, but his manner was gentle once he understood her situation and weariness. He moved like Abuela's gardener acquaintances. He didn't look like home, but his occupation felt like safety.

Delilah gave him the look she'd used on the mechanic's son. And she learned that the look worked no matter who the man was, no matter his age or size. The trick to the look was to imagine what you would do to reward the man should he please you – and keep the image in your thoughts as you held his gaze. Depending on the intuition of the man, and the vividness of his imagination – Delilah would learn over the next few months – this look worked within seconds to minutes. It worked now.

'I'll take you to the office,' he said. His face was no less stern, but he took her suitcase and offered her his free elbow. He made this move so awkwardly that Delilah recognized it as not something he was used to doing. She looped her arm through his and asked what the local soil, beyond the clay in that ditch he was clearing, was like.

By the time they reached the office, Martin had not only spoken fondly of the soil but had told her of a respectable boarding house where she could safely rent a room, and he recommended Delilah personally to the managing director of the Garden, who happened to be hanging around after a budget meeting.

'Delilah is exactly who we need in the ticket booth,' Martin said. And the managing director looked her up and down, and smiled in agreement.

Delilah hid her disappointment; but she'd bide her time before asking to be moved to grounds. During their trip to the boarding house when Martin got off work (he'd insisted on driving her there in his truck, shifting a bag of fertilizer and wiping down the seat with an almost-clean work shirt before helping her to climb in) Delilah learned that he was the married father of two small children. From then on, she referred to him as her 'uncle'. *Bien, mija. Bien*, Abuela told her that night when Delilah finally rested her tired head. *This is the way.*

To Espalier an Apple

After the handyman had finished digging out every second sand-stone slab from the backyard, moved them to the front garden to form a new path and smoothed the newly bereft holes left behind, he went away. Delilah had circled him like a feral cat meeting another cat in her particular alley the entire time he'd been on the property. Her hands clenched and unclenched when Roy handled her wheelbarrow, as if physically stopping herself from jerking it away.

Luckily, he'd brought his own shovel and crowbar, removing them from the small red truck he'd backed up the graveled drive; Delilah opened and closed the driveway chain for him. Delilah knew Anton watched from his window above as Roy arrived and departed. Anton no longer tried to hide, and with a strange man on her property, using her tools, his supervisory presence felt protective. Safe. Each time the driveway chain clinked into place, Anton's head nodded in satisfaction. With more tourists arriving on the island every day, Delilah assumed their plague-like descent explained Anton's vigilance. Mostly. Maybe.

The handyman, Roy, was almost completely silent and worked with an economy of movement. He was probably in his thirties, wore a thin wedding band and never once looked Delilah in the eye, although he, too, knew that Anton watched, and raised a hand in greeting. Delilah didn't mind Roy's avoidance of her person and direct gaze; in contrast, it made her feel powerful, like a Gorgon. When the job was completed, Roy accepted the cash she handed him with a muffled thanks and quickly drove away. Once she placed the chain in its proper position, Delilah ran back to the garden, grabbed a shovel and reclaimed her land.

The next week she spent on her knees, planting herbs she'd ordered from Island Hardware. Not only had she held endless discussions with Ted over the correct herbs to order, but she'd also placed a rare long-distance telephone call to Uncle Martin at the Garden to ask his advice. Oddly, he'd seemed quite emotional to hear from her. She shrugged this off as men being men (incomprehensible and prone to nostalgia), before bicycling over to the hardware store. She argued with Maisie Thompson over every single herb she wanted, but good-naturedly, almost. Maisie didn't seem to know how to interact without arguing, and Delilah found Maisie's personal antipathy to thyme entertaining. 'It stinks something awful,' Maisie ended. 'But if you want a stinky garden, that's your business.'

Delilah carefully separated the tender roots of the new herbs into smaller sections; these she placed into holes she scooped with her fingers in the freshly spaded and amended soil. She planted in the mornings after her run, not bothering to change into her overalls or washing the sweat from her face. What would be the point? Sometimes, still sweaty from her exertion, she drank from the garden hose, so unwilling was she to waste time entering the house for a glass. In the afternoons, tired and grimy, she walked around the garden, plotting. In the evenings, after bathing and changing (but still dressed for gardening, and wearing not the filmy underthings Alan expected, but instead the sensible cotton underpants that didn't pinch), she rode her bike to Ted's to report on each day's progress. He was always happy to see her, fancy pants or not. He was proud to hear of her progress in the herb garden, quick to suggest solutions for the placement of the admittedly stinky thyme. Ted's regard was so constant that she began to take him for granted. And she hardly noticed that it had nothing, or at least very little, to do with what she wore.

When Alan drove up that Friday, the foreign car crunching on the gravel after he opened the chain to gain entrance, Delilah raised a dazed face to his called-out greeting. She was in her overalls, on her knees, black earth under her nails and up to her elbows. Alan called again as she silently noted he didn't pull into her garage. No, he parked in the middle of the driveway as if he owned all of it, not merely half. Not even half of her half. It was all Alan's. Her annoyance at being interrupted, at his entitlement, was overcome by the metallic pang of panic when she noticed he hadn't bothered to close the chain behind his car. The driveway was exposed.

'Hi,' Alan said, standing above her, his tone impatient. 'I'm here.'

For a full thirty seconds there was no sign she even recognized Alan at all, let alone welcomed him. She didn't welcome him, she realized. She wanted him to go away. Then knowledge flooded her. This was Alan. He held expectations. Delilah had obligations. Her *job* was standing before her. Work-reddened cheeks flushed deeper as she scrambled to her feet; she was meant to be pleased to see him. He fended off her belated, muddy embrace, looking equally flustered. They retired, without speaking, into the house.

Inside the kitchen, Alan stood in the doorway leading to the enclosed stairs. He had to duck to walk up them and looked as if he were preparing to do so as he leaned there, head drooping to regard his tasseled loafers. Delilah left her boots on the porch, dropped her filthy overalls into the washing machine and washed her hands at the sink. She scrubbed under each nail with the snail-shaped brush. Her long-sleeved thermal undershirt was her only garment, but Alan didn't even raise his head.

'Let's get out of here,' he said. He shook his foot to watch the tassel dance.

'What?' Delilah turned off the water, splashing into the deep stone basin of the sink.

'I said...' He raised his face to look at hers. 'Let's get out of here.'

Delilah's wet hands dripped onto the floor. The drops splashed her feet, so she grabbed a towel and dried them, before squatting to wipe the floor. She threw the towel into the machine with her overalls. Cleaning calmed her. Maybe she'd mop the floor after putting Alan to bed. She hadn't actually heard what he said, surely. She didn't understand his meaning. His invitation was unprecedented.

'Let's go out to dinner in the city. Let's go home,' Alan said when she didn't immediately agree with his wishes. 'Spend the night. Maybe see a film. When is the last time we went out?'

Never, Delilah was careful not to say. *That would be never – since our first dates. You don't want to run into your friends, your family or, especially, your wife. We've never gone out as a couple.* She remained silent by biting her lip, then her tongue when his eyes moved to her mouth and he mirrored her, biting his own lip.

'Put your city clothes on, baby,' Alan said, seemingly encouraged by the lip-biting. As if she was trying to be provocative, not holding back her thoughts. 'Pack a bag, let's go.'

Delilah finally moved. She nodded in acknowledgment; she did not smile. She walked towards the stairs, but he stepped away quickly, obviously thinking she meant to embrace him in excitement at a night out or in gratitude for offering. Delilah was happy she was grubby from her daily toil. Alan was one of those men that only hugged his children when they were clean, she knew it.

'Take your time, baby,' Alan said. 'Have a bath. I'll make sure the place is locked up, maybe rest my eyes.'

Without a word or gesture, Delilah disappeared upstairs. She bathed; she dressed in her lacy, uncomfortable underthings and one of the flimsy dresses he had his secretary order for Delilah on her birthday and Christmas and Valentine's. She made up her face, painting on the red lipstick that Alan asked her to wear so she could leave smudged mouth marks all over his body. She packed a small bag before waking Alan from his deep slumber on the golden bed. Walking outside, he chatted about options of places to eat, seeing a show and getting a room. He put forth places in the city that no one he knew ever frequented. He never noticed that Delilah hadn't said a word. She didn't look up at the yellow house as she left the cottage. Alan didn't realize Delilah wasn't speaking, though her silence was as loud as she could project it.

She held the smallest overnight bag as she walked awkwardly in her high-heeled sandals through the gravel to ride shotgun in Alan's car. He'd never put the car into the garage, never closed the chain, so eager was he to remove her to neutral territory. Alan never knew how lucky he was that the unchained driveway hadn't been breached during their time in the house. And Delilah was relieved that on Friday nights Anton stayed in the kitchen, cooking elaborate meals and baking hard, crusty rolls of bread, far away from his window perch guarding the driveway and what went on beyond it. Or, rather, she told herself that what she was feeling was relief. She was almost certain of it. It most definitely was not a longing to be rescued; Delilah was not that kind of girl.

That night, after they left the ferry, Alan drove them far out of the city on the mainland, on the dark country roads with the car top open to the starry night sky, to the type of tourist town that was full of antique stores, diners pretending to be pubs, and bed-and-breakfast inns instead of motels. Normally, Delilah would be enchanted and want to explore – she'd seen these types of towns on Sunday afternoon matinees on television while eating popcorn and listening to Abuela judge everyone's behavior, but she hadn't imagined she'd get to visit one in person. However, now she was preoccupied by her unfinished garden waiting for her back home, bothered by the greasy feel of the make-up that Alan preferred her to wear and no longer accustomed to her city shoes pinching her toes. She worried about the driveway, left with only Anton to guard it. She didn't know if he'd seen her leave, or if he'd known about the brief time when the driveway was assailable. She didn't want him to blame her for Alan's carelessness.

Her preoccupation kept her quiet and, for the first time, the fact that Alan enjoyed her silence bothered her. His air of entitlement to this silence made her seethe. If Delilah knew how, if it hadn't been bred out of her for safety reasons, she would have loved to pick a fight. Alas, it was not in her nature. She resented that, too.

Alan didn't ask her what she wanted to eat; he ordered for her. He didn't ask if she'd like a bite of his steak; he cut a piece and pushed it into her mouth. When he finished eating, although Delilah was still picking at her salmon, he stood and led her upstairs to their room. Delilah was bone-weary. She'd been gardening since dawn on her hands and knees, had forgotten to eat lunch but didn't care for the sweet flesh of this pink fish, and had rushed from her home at Alan's bidding. She was longing to scrub her face free from the make-up and fall into the bed covered with feather pillows and billowing quilts. She did do all that, but Alan was in the bed, too. Alan had expectations. Alan could go to hell.

The most Delilah offered was a sleepy 'goodnight' before she turned her back to him and snuggled into the comfortable mattress. She felt Alan's stiffened shock and outrage for a moment, but she was truly exhausted so she sighed once, deeply, before slumber pulled her in and she felt no more. Abuela had spoken of the sleep of the righteous, but the sleep of righteous indignation was pretty wonderful, too. *Alan can lump it* was her last conscious thought.

In the morning, used to rising before the sun, Delilah bathed and dressed in order to be downstairs eating breakfast before he woke. Alan arrived, looking extremely displeased. So thunderous was his expression that Delilah spared a thought for his wife. If Teresa had to put up with this mood every morning, she had all of Delilah's sympathy. This benevolence on her part kept Delilah cheerful through Alan's surly eating, and through their packing and departure.

'I'll let you travel on alone,' Alan said when they reached the ferry landing and he removed her bag from the car. 'Since you're so obviously *not* in the mood to be with me.'

Delilah leaned across the small suitcase he'd dropped at her feet, wrapped her arms around his neck – forcing him to catch her or send them both toppling to the ground – and kissed him in a manner deeply inappropriate to the time and the public arena. Every ounce of benevolent sympathy for Teresa, every frustration at being removed from her garden without a by-your-leave, every drop of anger at Alan's supposed grievance and demands, it all went into the kiss she gave him. She added a final sharp nip of his bottom lip as she stepped away. Alan pulled his jacket hastily closed. She'd rendered him mute and left him bloody.

'Goodbye, my darling,' Delilah said. She picked up the suitcase and walked to the ferry queue. 'I hope you feel better soon.'

She never looked back to see Alan's reaction or departure. As she found a seat for the crossing, her weirdly high spirits wore off, calmed down, dissolved in the sunlight thrown back at her from the sea waves, and she spent the rest of the trip worrying about what she'd find awaiting her in the driveway, in the garden and her home. It was a somber Delilah who reached the island.

Her city shoes were not meant for long walks, so she kicked them off once she disembarked from the ferry. Ted found her this way, barefoot in a silly dress and carrying an overnight bag. He drove her to the cottage in his cruiser. She climbed into the vehicle with a wry wink as a greeting. It was embarrassment at decent Ted seeing her in this condition that kept her quiet, not angry indignation. It was the first time she'd ever felt any shame regarding her relationship to Alan.

'He's just a job,' she wanted to tell Ted. 'He doesn't mean anything.'

But she knew even an employer shouldn't treat her the way Alan had that morning. No one should treat another person as an object designed to be used and put away, forgotten until it was needed again. Delilah chose to ignore that this was almost exactly how she felt about Alan as well. It wouldn't do anyone any good if she started facing truths right now. And she figured Ted would be uncomfortable with the truth of her statement anyway. If Alan was just a job, what was Ted?

At the shared driveway, as she stood in the gravel connecting her home to the yellow house, she was so deep in her thoughts, her silence, that she only remembered to thank Ted when he'd started to drive away, left arm hanging from his open window.

'See you later?' she asked in addition, tentative for the first time in their relationship. The air smelled of salt water, tomatoes, roasted garlic and the acid flavor of rosemary in olive oil. Delilah's mouth filled with saliva and her eyes stung. 'Ted?'

'Of course.' Ted waved goodbye, his arm no longer hanging forlornly.

Upstairs in the yellow house a window banged shut. Ted drove off when Delilah was safely inside the cottage. She heard his tires leave the gravel before she went upstairs to change and bathe her feet. Afterwards, she and Ted never talked about that meeting. It was like the morning walk and silent drive had never taken place. Ted didn't like to think where she'd been and with whom, and Delilah... Delilah was starting to have thoughts that were best left unmentioned for now.

*

Delilah finished the herb garden in record time, fearing more interruptions. Resenting them in advance. The fury with which she worked was about more than interruptions, being pulled away; an urgency rode her. Sometimes she felt like its puppet as she watched her own hands perform tasks she'd done all her life. She felt it, but that was all. She didn't know enough yet to name it, so she called it concern for the job at hand, for her garden. Planted, mulched and gently watered, it was beautiful.

In six months, when the greenery filled in the bare spots to overlap the soft beige sandstone, it would be prettier still. Delilah took a photo of what she had done and then stood motionless, feeling abandoned. What was she supposed to do now with the feeling building inside her? Where was all the energy to go? She looked up, beyond the herbs, beyond the sandstone steps and the delicate white wrought-iron table and chairs Ted had given her from his own garden, to the willows that covered the fence. She saw that the willows were sad, raggedy excuses for trees, and realized that they had to go.

She was still standing there, staring, filing through various tree options in her mind (had he but known), when Anton finished his run. He came up the beach path, loose and relaxed from the exertion – for once not thinking, merely tired from doing – but paused when he spied his beautiful neighbor staring into space. Or rather, into trees.

It didn't even seem odd to Anton anymore, the things she did. Standing statue-still for minutes on end, staring at some kind of sad tree in her yard? Sure, for her it was completely normal. She was so goofy; it was an excellent thing she was also beautiful. Then he spied the camera. He should really go inside, on the off chance she got trigger-happy with that thing. Anton shook his head at his own ridiculousness, but the camera disturbed him, until he understood that the herb garden was finished and she was recording her achievement. Anton remembered photographing the first successful cheesecake he'd ever produced and found his feet moving towards Delilah. Poor kid, with no one to share with – for her he'd take the risk.

Hearing the crunch of the gravel, Delilah woke from her reverie. She didn't turn to look at him, but pointed into the garden. 'Thanks for Roy,' she said. 'Look.'

'Looks nice.' Anton was sincere, although 'nice' was too tame a word. The herb garden was elegant and charming, a perfect spot for morning tea or an evening glass of wine, but Anton was afraid of becoming too honest with her. To maintain distance, he mentally added an outdoor patio to his imaginary restaurant, his game that he hadn't needed to play since Delilah's arrival. But the couple enjoying their glasses of wine while sharing a cannolo were looking a little too familiar, and Anton jerked his mind to Delilah's garden, here in the present, away from his fantasy. He took a step back from her. He couldn't risk being so close to her. He was afraid to be his true self – the self who wasn't Anton.

'Roy did a good job, although I think I scared him.' She didn't seem concerned.

'His name is Ray,' Anton said. Hadn't she read the card?

'He said Roy.'

'No, he said Ray, because that's his name, and you misheard.' Why wouldn't she look at him?

'Is everyone on this island lying about their name?' Delilah asked. She was staring into the rough willows at the fence line.

'Why?' Anton's attention was caught. 'What's your real name?'

'Dolores,' Delilah said. 'Can you imagine? I'm named for my grandmother, my abuela. I changed it as soon as I could.'

'Lola?' Anton asked jokingly and he swore she shuddered.

'Not Lola,' she said. 'Never Lola.'

'You *do* look like a Dolores,' Anton said. 'Not a Lola, you're right.'

She jerked her head to stare at him, not liking his statement. He had to study her closely, like he'd just met her: Dolores. Or maybe like he'd had a head injury... *Stop staring at her.* She grimaced at him. She looked as though she'd like to smack him. God help him, he'd enjoy even a slap from her. He killed his responding smile before its birth. He needed to stop staring at her. He was afraid that for her he'd ruin everything.

'I do not,' she said. '*Stop* it. And don't tell anyone.'

Anton laughed an abrupt snort. 'Who would I tell? I don't talk to anyone.'

'Don't tell Alan,' Delilah said. 'Or...'

'Huh.' Anton started to walk away. 'I don't even know who that is.'

Delilah was left standing in the driveway, her mouth half-open. Anton was pleased; proud that he was able to walk away, leaving her looking so frustrated. He liked her mean. Maybe he could provoke her to the point she would slap him; he couldn't remember the last time he'd been touched.

'The garden really does look nice,' Anton said again, almost at his deck. He spoke to her over his shoulder. 'See you around, Dolores.'

He heard a sharp thunk, like she'd kicked a stone, but when he turned back to take one last look at her annoyed face from the top of his deck stairs, she'd gone.

Ted came to see the garden, a bit nervous because Delilah had waved him in when he'd been driving by in the cruiser. He was on duty, but he couldn't resist her smile or the enthusiastic gesture of her beckoning arm. He was worried that lines were being blurred. Maybe he should have worried about that sooner. Before. Before *what*, he didn't want to admit. He wondered who was watching, as the sound of the gravel crunching under the cruiser's tires made him cringe.

All watching eyes were forgotten when Delilah took him by the hand to drag him to the area behind the cottage. She wanted him to see what she had made. His wife's ill health had prevented them from having children, but Ted had always wanted to be a father. In the current situation this thought made Ted extremely uncomfortable and he banished it. He was glad he had when, once behind the screen of the cottage, Delilah threw her arms around his neck and kissed him in a definitely non-daughterly way.

When she pulled back, her eyes were looking over his shoulder, like she was staring at someone. Someone with whom she was unhappy. The back of his neck tingling, Ted turned. But there was no one in the driveway. They were alone.

'The garden is finished, I see,' he said, turning back to it. 'Beautiful job.'

'Yes, it is! Thanks for figuring out the logistics.' She patted him solicitously on the arm. In doing so she bumped her elbow on his service revolver and shied away. 'Now, turn your mind to this problem.'

She pointed to the willows, and then opened her palm in a questioning, almost exasperated, gesture.

'What? The trees?' he asked. He walked closer to where the trees obscured the fence. He reached through the tangled branches, pushing them aside, in order to thump the wooden fence behind them.

'The trees aren't hurting the fence,' he said, and Delilah frowned. He grinned at her frustration. 'They aren't hurting the fence because it's cedar. Mr Oakapple next door believed in building to last.'

Delilah was entirely uninterested in the neighbors with whom she did not share a driveway and her face reflected this. She wanted to be rid of the ugly, tangled willows, but she also believed in preserving trees wherever possible. She wanted Ted to solve her problem for her. She tilted her head and gave him the look that hit him every time. This look worked within seconds to turn his mind to pure animal instinct, to make him understand he existed only to please her. It worked now.

'Cedar is pretty, too,' Ted said, flushing and shifting in his stance. He moved back to her side to take her hand. 'Without the willows you'd see the red wood.'

Delilah smiled encouragingly and gently patted his hand with her free one, before drifting away. Ted moved with her. Even distracted, the couple stepped carefully to avoid the delicate herbs settling in the soil.

'Cedar is wonderful for espaliering,' Ted said, still seeking her. 'It is an herb garden. You could espalier a fruit tree to the fence. I have apple trees!'

Delilah saw the idea seed in his mind's eye. He released her gaze in order to turn and study the fence, the willows, the amount of sunlight reaching them. She saw his gardening instinct win out over lust. She hugged her arms around her waist. She loved older men.

'Ted,' she said and he immediately turned to her, giving her that brief, brilliant smile she also loved, before his face settled back into its wrinkled squint of concentration. 'What's your real name?'

'Theodore,' he said. He turned back to the gardening idea at hand, not curious in the slightest about why she'd asked. She didn't look at the house behind her.

'I have two baby apple trees I grew from seed,' Ted continued, pacing off the fence line. He was stepping carefully on the stones. 'Have you ever espaliered a tree?'

Delilah shook her head. She smiled again, a satisfied smile now, verging on triumphant, and sat down on the steps of her cottage. Cat-like, she lifted her face to the sun and, only coincidentally, to the window of the yellow house next door. 'Tell me about it,' she said.

The morning after Anton watched Delilah kissing the sheriff (and what was *that* about?), he finished his run at the same moment that Delilah, coming from the opposite direction, finished hers. They didn't speak. Delilah jerked her head sideways before heading down the path, expecting him to follow. Anton did. Not only did he live down the path anyway, but she had a look on her face that... *What?* he asked himself. What was it about her face?

Anton wanted to know what she wanted from him; it was as simple as that. But nothing in life is ever as simple as that. Delilah was filling two glasses from a pitcher of water on her wrought-iron table. The pitcher was made of ceramic, marbled pink with a large blue rose. It reminded Anton of something his nonna might have used. The glasses were regular juice glasses, but she'd put a lace doily on the tray. Clearly, she'd planned this visit.

She took her glass and sat on the porch steps, where she picked up a waiting coffee-table book. Anton tried to resent that he'd been set up as he grabbed the glass meant for him and joined her on the steps. He should resent that she knew he would do as she bid. But she patted the wooden top step next to her and, God help him, all Anton felt was wanted.

Delilah placed the book on his lap. He drained the water from his glass before handing it to her. She gave it a glance before setting it behind her. Anton understood that she wasn't going to serve him. He grinned. It made him so smug when she was mean. She wasn't mean to strangers.

She ignored his high spirits and flipped open the book to a marked page. She pointed.

'Look,' she said. She sounded horrified.

The page read *To Espalier an Apple* and it gave step-by-step instructions next to detailed photographs. Anton studied the page, then flipped to the next one. Delilah averted her eyes to focus on the willow trees.

'The willows are ugly,' Delilah said. 'I want them gone, but...'

'You can't bring yourself to crucify an apple tree?' Anton winced at the photograph depicting a hole being drilled through a slender branch in order to anchor it to the wired fence behind it.

'I guess it looks elegant when it's done and all,' Delilah turned the page to examine the final photograph, 'but I don't think I can do it. I can't split and cut and drill baby branches and screw them to a fence.'

'I take it someone else thinks you should?'

Delilah nodded. She pulled the rubber band from her hair and let the black curtain fall down to obscure her face from his view.

'So don't do it,' Anton said, closing the book. He handed it back to her. 'It's your garden, your call.'

'What do you do in there?' she asked him. Their hands brushed against each other, once and then twice, before they slowly moved away. 'What do you do all day?'

Anton, caught unawares, heard himself responding. He watched her hands, now smoothing over the cover of the book on her lap. Again and again, she stroked it. He heard his voice from a great distance.

'I'm writing a book,' his voice said. 'It's not a cookbook. And I'm planning my restaurant.'

'Why isn't it a cookbook?' Delilah must have been interested, because she pushed her hair back in order to examine his face.

'Because...' *Stop talking*, he told the stranger named Anton. 'Because it's a memoir.'

'Oh, I see,' Delilah said in a tone that told him she did not see at all. 'What's your real name?'

Then Anton's self-preservation or muscle memory or just common sense kicked in. *Why would she ask that?* He stopped talking, giving up information, but he couldn't stop staring at her. She was sitting so close. Her black hair was curling in sweaty wisps at her temples, her earlobe was pierced but empty, and her nutmeg-colored irises stared back at him, bemused. *What harm would it do to tell her the truth?*

Here was a conundrum, though. Was Anton the one thinking this? Or was Delilah? Were they thinking each other's thoughts once more? Maybe telling her the truth would do a lot of harm, maybe none at all. Anton was beginning to lose sight of his boundaries, his goals. He summoned a picture of his marshal's long-suffering face at their last meeting, which didn't help much. Anton pictured his nonna disappointed in him when his manicotti dissolved into an inedible mess. This snapped him right out of his enthrallment. Delilah was waiting. Let her wait.

She flipped the black hair aside to look at him. He wiped the sweat off his brow with the back of one hand. She was still looking at him. He was thirsty and obviously she wasn't going to offer him another glass of water. He reached behind her to snag his glass. She didn't move and he was forced to lean in much closer to her than he'd meant to. The warmth pouring off her body – freshly exercised, still dewy with exertion – reminded him of all the kitchens he'd ever been in; he wanted to roll in it, set dough to rise on her lap. He longed to wrap his entire self around her. He'd been alone in the yellow house a very long time. She raised her nose and inhaled the air above his neck, close to his ear, before delicately releasing her breath in a soft sigh. She hadn't stopped looking at him.

Anton grabbed the glass, his face mere inches from Delilah's, and stood up. He poured water from the pitcher and drained it from the glass without pausing for breath. Her silence only added to the discomfort of her nearness and warmth. They were no longer hearing each other's thoughts, if they ever had been. Anton felt it like a loss. Anton suffered.

'Have you checked the chain this morning?' he asked her and she shook her head. He leaped from the herb garden and started around the cottage, calling over his shoulder as he left her: 'You have to be diligent or they will get in.'

Walking away to check the chain gave him a chance to calm down and break the lock she had on him with her stare. The chain was there, still in place; everything was fine. Anton did need to break her stare, didn't he? He held two goals on this island: keep the tourists out of his driveway and not get involved with the locals.

Delilah, though – she wasn't really a local. She didn't even want to nail a tree to a fence. She had an abuela; she lied about her name. She didn't belong here any more than he did. And she smelled like salty vanilla and her body heat was like bread fresh from the oven. Anton started walking back. Maybe she'd like to stare at him some more. Anton thought he'd sensed a certain promise in that stare. Perhaps there was promise in that sniff she'd taken of his neck. He could offer her more.

When he went around the corner of the cottage, however, the steps were empty. The pitcher and water glasses were gone. The book on how to espalier an apple tree lay abandoned on the top step, its pages ruffling in the bite of the sea breeze that rampaged over the dunes and up the driveway between their separate buildings. Anton went home. He was filled with a sudden desire to bake bread and make cheesecake. Vanilla cheesecake. He'd put flaked salt on top.

In Alan's City

Within a few months, even Martin the head groundskeeper no longer remembered that Delilah was not really his niece. Or at least, this is what he told Mrs Martin when she finally met Delilah at the Garden's open day for employees' families. After watching Delilah, overalled knees stained green and a dirt smudge on one cheek, teach her eldest girl to make a daisy necklace while giving baby Martin his bottle on the tussocky grass, Mrs Martin settled back to a peaceful picnic and never said peep when little Mariah called the pretty young thing Cousin Delilah. Her Martin was a good family man.

Teaching the children to make daisy necklaces or roll down the gentle hills of the Garden's rare grass exhibit, and feeding Martin Jr while his mother ate, kept all the adolescent sons and husbands with wandering eyes (and possibly hands) at a safe distance. Messy-haired, overalled Delilah, shielded by a bevy of little girls and with her arms full of a fat baby fathered by the scariest man in the Garden, found herself enjoying a visit with another woman for the first time since she'd left the Violet Lady sleeping on the bus. Mrs Martin reminded Delilah of a grown-up Rosario, capable and calm and secure in her place in the world. She wore motherhood like an almost visible mantle of respectability. When Uncle Martin looked at his wife, it was very much like the way his baby son looked at her – like he stared at the entire universe.

Only, with Martin Sr there was a touch of fear; Delilah admired Mrs Martin for that especially.

'Mrs Dowling?' Mrs Martin asked as they watched the replete baby fall asleep on the blanket between them. 'The boarding house by the estuary? Isn't it damp? It's so rickety! I expect to hear it's fallen down after every storm.'

'It's fine,' Delilah said. She was braiding another chain for Mariah – the little girl wanted a tiara now. 'It's not too damp.'

'My niece...' Mrs Martin stopped. 'My sister's daughter, she needs another roommate. One of her current ones, I can't keep track of them, is getting married.'

'Mrs Dowling's is fine,' Delilah said again. But she smiled without showing her teeth and kept her eyes vulnerable when not downturned to her work.

'Hannah's apartment is in such a nice part of town – the more girls to split the rent, the merrier.' Mrs Martin was obviously pleased with her plans for everyone and everything; Delilah saw that it was futile to argue with her. It was easier to just go along, allow her to arrange new living quarters for her 'niece'.

Uncle Martin, approaching to claim a second sandwich, looked approvingly on as Mrs Martin wrote down the particulars for Delilah and told her she'd talk with her niece... her niece Hannah, that was. Delilah took the paper ripped from Mrs Martin's checkbook, nodded in acquiescence and bid her proper thanks.

Delilah was moving her belongings into Hannah's apartment – after months in the city she owned two suitcases, a large potted fern and a box of kitchen accoutrements – when she lost control of the precarious arrangement and dropped it all at a man's feet. She saved the fern by clasping it to her breast. The passerby was older, well-dressed, his hair a little longer than was respectable. *That's interesting.* Delilah took the time to give him the once-over as she heard Abuela whisper, *He thinks rules don't apply to him and he must have the money to back his belief.* His eyes were kind, though. He helped her collect the implements from the spilled box and rearrange the cases under her arms, with the fern in one hand to be easily carried, and tipped a nonexistent hat at her before he climbed into his expensive car parked at the curb and pulled away. Delilah promptly forgot him.

Delilah's promotion to garden assistant, working mostly under the direction of Uncle Martin, meant she was no longer confined to the suffocating ticket booth. Dealing with the public – selling tickets, answering questions and dodging the flirtations of men – was not what Delilah had in mind the day she asked Martin for help obtaining work at the Garden.

While Delilah's appearance made her the perfect addition to the front gate, her shyness and the line that developed when men tried to get more than a ticket and a map from her were not plus points in the mind of Mrs Bacchus, the supervisor. The Garden had never really had lines before – even on weekends, traffic meandered through so slowly that the entrance had no infrastructure to welcome more than a handful of people at a time – so when the first man leaned in to rest his elbow on the counter in an attempt to sweet-talk Delilah into walking with him, the delay caused a ruckus.

'Could you maybe show me to the duck pond?' asked the middle-aged man with a rolled-up newspaper in the pocket of his suit. (*Only drifters keep a spare newspaper handy, mija. Drifters or perverts. Cuidate!* Abuela was abruptly standing next to Delilah, her arms crossed, her sharpest triangular weeder in her hand.) 'It's my first time here. Don't you offer tours? I read that in the brochure, right?'

Delilah recognized the ploy of the multiple questions; he thought he could force a response or she'd feel impolite. She was not a girl who felt impolite. Did this drifter not know that her beauty gave her power? Delilah became icy in consequence.

She took a step away to pivot around the counter and make eye contact with the guard across the way – so unaccustomed to actually *guarding* that he sat on the mushroom roof of a small ceramic Japanese teahouse and read a paperback warped by the moist, salty air – to demand with her big brown eyes and tightly frowning lips that he immediately come to her aid. At her request, and to the utter outrage of the newspaper-pocket man, he did. The guard took the man's elbow off the counter and walked him down the path, all the while giving him the worst possible directions to ensure that the man only found the duck pond by accident, hopefully by falling face-first into its murk. Delilah crossed her fingers and helped the next customer. Sadly, he was another lone male, somehow emboldened by the first man's failure. Delilah missed her hatpin. By the fourth entitled man, she would have settled for Abuela's garden hoe.

The guard took up position next to the counter instead of sitting back on the little house, but this was also nerve-wracking because when the stream of visitors slowed during the late afternoon lull, he wanted to chat. Delilah was not used to chatting with older men who read quasi-pornographic dime-store novels in public and insisted on telling her the plot points; she did not wish to become used to it, she knew by the end of the day. Thank heavens for mothers with small children and nannies with strollers and teenagers cutting class – if it had been men all day, Delilah would have stabbed someone without question. Or at least whacked them strongly with the old cast-iron stapler she used to attach their receipt to the map of the Garden.

Mrs Bacchus saw her exhaustion at the end of the first day and frowned, which Delilah and the guard both interpreted as displeasure with *her*. But Mrs Bacchus had been young once, and while she'd never been pretty, she'd worked in service all her life. The supervisor moved the reading guard to the exit gate at the other end of the Garden, and placed the happily married – rather stern, not so prone to glad-handing people – younger guard to the front, next to Delilah's counter. She encouraged both of her new gatekeepers to be as unsmiling as they needed to be. It only helped a little. Delilah was so lovely in the sunlight and cool breeze, the sweet scents of the Garden surrounding her, that even the happily married guard was tempted to be less stern and the lines of single male visitors only increased, as somehow word got out of the young beauty in the Garden. Mrs Bacchus spent more time at the front gate than she ever had before; she was almost in despair and quite glad her own daughters were really rather plain.

When Delilah asked again and again to be moved to Grounds and the lines of men increased, finally Mrs Bacchus overcame years of ingrained gender norms and turned her over to Uncle Martin, who was Head of Grounds. Only the returning male visitors were disappointed. Delilah outdoors, on the grounds, was in her element. Instead of the prim dress covered with a slightly fussy apron that she'd worn at the gate, she dressed in chambray work shirts under baggy overalls with pockets and a loop upon which to hang her razor-sharp shears. Delilah felt safer, more complete, with those shears bumping her upper thigh at every step of her thick-soled work boots. With Uncle Martin, her direct and only supervisor, nearby in case of unexpected questions or company, and the work of upkeep and planting never-ending, Delilah was closer to content than she'd ever been in her young, upheaval-ridden life.

The day Delilah met Alan, met him properly, she was separating amaryllis bulbs from those crowding a sidewalk bed and depositing them into brown paper bags to be sold in the Garden's gift shop. It was the work she most loved, found the most soothing; relieving the stress on the amaryllis, neatening the bed and giving the rejected plants purpose – all done in the slightly salty breeze and the fresh, warm sunlight. Delilah was so satisfied as she kneeled in the fragrant, loamy soil that she didn't hear his footsteps and was quite startled when a throat was cleared above her.

She had been contemplating slipping one or two bulbs into the pocket of her overalls, although she had no garden, so maybe it was a slightly guilty conscience that had caused her to jerk in startlement and her cheeks to flush. Whatever the cause, she felt even more flustered when he said, 'Hello, Delilah.'

When her eyes only widened in response, and she rose from her knees in preparation to flee, he gestured to the name tag pinned to her overalls' strap. She didn't run to Uncle Martin after all, but neither did she get back on her knees to finish the work.

'What are you doing here?' the man asked, gesturing to the disrupted garden bed behind her with the unpeeled orange he held. Delilah remembered him now – his too-long-for-staidness hair and his kind brown eyes.

'I work here,' Delilah said. At his indulgent smile, she blushed deeper. Of course he knew that; it was most likely why he was there. 'These amaryllis need separating to flourish and we sell the extra bulbs in the Garden shop.'

As Delilah continued to explain the procedure in depth, thinking to share her expertise and pleasure, the man peeled the orange with a tiny silver pocketknife. Delilah had a Leatherman tool hanging from her overalls' loop that could peel the orange and also take off a limb (from tree or man), but she didn't think mentioning that would endear her to the man. When Delilah ran out of explanation, it was only natural to step out of the rumpled amaryllis patch, sit on a nearby bench with the man and eat the juicy pieces of fruit he handed her.

'My name is Alan,' he said. 'I work nearby – actually, my office overlooks the Garden – but I've seen you before.'

'Yes,' Delilah said between bites. 'I remember.'

He smiled, pleased. Delilah held in her sigh and kept her eyes locked on her fruit segment so that they didn't roll at all. He stretched his long arms over the back of the bench, his fingers not quite brushing her right shoulder. He was still preening a little at her remembering him. 'The Garden is my favorite spot for a peaceful break during the day.' That made sense to Delilah – the Garden was the best spot in the entire city, after all.

Together they finished the orange and then Alan offered Delilah his handkerchief to clean her hands. He told her he hoped to see her again, before departing in a correctly polite manner. Delilah stayed on the bench for a moment: her knees could use the break and she could use the time to ruminate on possible stratagems. How could he be useful to her?

Only a young girl raised by Abuela was capable of looking right through Alan and his very pretty gentlemanly behavior. Abuela might as well have stood behind Delilah's seat on the wrought-iron bench, murmuring Spanish deprecations and advice. Indeed, as Alan disappeared around the bend at the bottom of the hill with a final jaunty wave, Delilah quite clearly heard Abuela's voice on the ocean-scented breeze: *Engaña a quien te engaña que en este mundo todo es magaña.* A rhyme that didn't translate well, but meant something like: 'Deceive those who deceive you, for in this world everything is a trick.'

The car Alan climbed into that first day was an expensive one. His clothes screamed money; even his posture denoted privilege. He'd made no overt demands or assumptions of Delilah. In fact, he'd fed her. He didn't wear a wedding ring, and he had an office in a luxury building overlooking the Garden. Alan was very rich; he had pretty manners; he obviously wanted her; he looked like security.

Delilah had been cold, scared and alone in Mrs Dowling's boarding house. Even now, with roommates in her new digs, she felt alone and frequently anxious about the future. What if she were hurt or ill? Who would care for her? Who, really, would care at all? Alan, with his gentle eyes, cutting fruit for her with his silver knife, looked like safety. He looked like someone who could pay for the home she wanted to create. Delilah, alone now for almost a year, pushed down her misgivings and resolved to try to trust Alan. He'd looked into her eyes with such sweetness, after all.

Delilah knew Alan would return. What could possibly stop him from attempting to take what he wanted? There were a separate set of rules for rich white men. She would be delightfully surprised when he arrived. Hesitantly pleased to take him up on his offer to spend time together. She'd agree to his plans, as long as they were respectable; she'd be sweet and biddable until the point his suggestions were no longer so innocent, and they entered into open negotiations. Then she would take him for anything – and everything – he had. As stratagems went, it was a simple one.

The Path at the End of
the Driveway

Summer cracked open and the ferry poured forth its river of tourists. They came by foot and car, filling every available hotel room and rentable edifice. The Bradshaws further down Mulberry Street parked their car at the curb, shoved two sets of bunk beds in the garage and made enough money to pay for a new bathroom, but most islanders found that crass. Ray Ramirez told Ted all about it. The Bradshaws had hired Ray to put in the framework for the new ceiling. They were paying him under the table because they hadn't bothered to get the proper permits. People were forever telling Ted things he'd just as soon not know.

Ted was so busy patrolling, citing, settling ticket disputes and answering self-evident questions from wandering visitors that he had no time for his own personal visitor. His garden was suffering, too. Delilah started going over every other day to do a little work in the neglected space. She was a love of a girl. She left harvested vegetables on his kitchen table, along with little notes. Once she left a slightly squashed slice of delicious cheesecake, which surprised him. He hadn't known she baked. She picked the ripe fruit and vegetables in his temporarily abandoned garden, she watered, she brought in his mail and left it in a neat pile by the telephone, but Ted hadn't seen her in days. He missed her. He'd never become attached to an off-islander before.

When the dispatcher radioed in Delilah's address and said she'd called in a trespass complaint, Ted was actually looking forward to seeing her, even if it was in his official capacity. He'd take her in any capacity he could.

Delilah was pacing at the mouth of her driveway, her cheeks an agitated red even without weekend make-up. She wasn't wearing her overalls but a pair of cut-off jeans and a skimpy camisole top. She looked like the students and the youngsters who should be students but weren't that the evening news on television featured more and more. This reminded Ted of her age, and he dropped the comparison. But even aggravated, she was lovely.

Delilah's downy upper lip was beaded with moisture from the heat. She wiped it off with the back of her hand while she explained to Ted why she was upset. Her black hair was not in its usual ponytail but hanging in loose, messy curls. It had grown so long that when she pushed it back, she needed to use her entire forearm, reaching under the thick black heaviness at her neck to sweep it up and pull the curls away from her damp cheeks. Ted realized she'd never cut it since moving in; he would have heard the gossip had she gone to the local beauty salon. Her hair now reached almost to her waist. He moved to stroke it when it fell back, tangled, as she dropped the mass again in order to tug her camisole down decently, but he stopped his hand before he could touch it. He only wanted to calm her, mostly, but he was on duty.

'They must have undone the chain, see? It was here on the ground when I came home,' Delilah was saying. The chain was back in place, but the damage was done. Two cars were parked in the graveled drive, one blocking the garage of the yellow house. 'Anton is going to be so upset. He always says tourists are like locusts.'

Ted didn't quite follow the last sentence, and he wasn't sure how he felt about Delilah quoting what her neighbor 'always said'.

How much time did she spend with him? How many conversations had they had for her to know the man's idioms? Since when did she even know his name? Ted hadn't known the man's name until she told him. His professional pride was hurt, that's all, he told himself. It was not jealousy that motivated him; it was not possessiveness. Ted knew he was lying to himself.

'How long have they been here?' Ted finally gave in and touched her, running one hand down her arm. He told himself this was to gain her attention. She hadn't stopped pacing.

'I don't know. After ten?' She shrugged, before pushing her hair back again. He wished he had a hair tie to offer her. Of all the things he wished to offer her, for the moment a hair tie was the most relevant.

'I've been at your place, watering, and then I stopped to trade vegetables for eggs from Maisie Thompson – which was a big mistake because the store was packed – and then I got here and the chain was torn down and cars parked. Do you think you can have them towed before Anton gets home? He'll be so angry they've blocked his garage.'

'Towed?' Ted was startled. 'Usually, I just hunt down the owners and ask them...'

'There's no time for that,' Delilah said, grabbing his hands. She threaded her fingers through his and gave both hands a little shake. 'And really, these people need to be taught a lesson.'

Ted, having never seen this side of Delilah's personality, was experiencing a surreal moment. She was a territorial person. He was not allowed in her house because another man paid for it. Fine, he understood that. (He was beginning to hate the other man and plot means of removing him from Delilah's life, but that was a thought for another day.) Yet Delilah wasn't upset because she'd come home to tourists trespassing and leaving their cars on *her* property. She was angry and territorial on behalf of a neighbor whom Ted hadn't known she even talked to, let alone knew well enough to call him by his first name – let alone well enough to quote him while calling him by name. The last time they'd spoken of the man, she'd known nothing about him; when had this all *happened*? Ted felt out of the loop.

This was ridiculous – he was the sheriff. People needed to respect his position. His neck tightened, and he cracked it with a shrug and a twist, then freed his hands from hers to adjust his belt and straightened to his full height, chest thrust out.

Damn right Ted was going to have the tourists' cars towed. Then he was going to find the tourists and cite them for trespassing. He hoped they were the loud, entitled types who tried to intimidate and throw their weight around, because Ted would welcome an excuse to react in a hostile, aggressive manner. Ted felt like Delilah had looked when he arrived: very agitated. He hadn't felt this agitated in years, now that he thought about it. He welcomed an opportunity to take his animus out on someone.

Delilah must have sensed this, because she stopped pacing, gave him the once-over, and then looked satisfied. 'Do you want to come in and use my telephone?'

'No, I'll radio from the cruiser.' Ted shot a glare of pure venom at the Camaro blocking the yellow house's garage.

Delilah caught him by surprise then. She stepped up on her barefoot tiptoes, pressed against him with her arms around his neck and slid her tongue fully into his mouth to rub against his own like a sauntering cat marking a fence post. Once, twice her tongue rewarded him and then she ended with an absurdly chaste peck on his lips before she pulled away. It was a bright afternoon, fully public, and he was on duty. She moved away, nonchalant as anything, walking over to her front porch to sit on the steps and finger-comb her hair in preparation for braiding. She looked up at him, standing where she'd left him, and tilted her chin towards his cruiser in encouragement. Ted, completely discombobulated, retreated to his vehicle.

Ted was born and raised on the island. He had only ever gone away to go to the police academy. He'd returned and got married, but he'd only ever had two interests: his work and his garden. Gladys was a socially expected accompaniment to his life, and he'd always assumed that he loved her. They were both disappointed when they didn't have children. They were devastated when she got cancer. Ted was flattened when she died. But Ted realized he couldn't remember her face now, and the love he'd felt for Gladys was a pale flame in comparison to the blue-white heat of his passion for Delilah.

The last time he and Delilah were together – before the onslaught of the tourists had begun – Ted, prostrate in his torn-apart bed, thought he might be having a heart attack. The muscle was beating in a syncopated rhythm similar to the noise his old Bronco made right before its carburetor gave out. He was unable to catch his breath. Delilah was sitting up, sipping water; she looked sleepy.

'I think you might be the death of me,' Ted said when he could speak. Delilah put down her glass of water, flipped on her side and slid down in the bed in order to face him. 'I wouldn't mind – death by Delilah would be worth it.' Ted's heartbeat settled into a calmer pace.

Delilah laughed. She looked fully awake now, sleepiness banished by what, exactly, Ted couldn't imagine. Worry for Ted's imminent doom? Pleasure in his compliment? Pride in having him completely at her mercy? Sheriff Ted held no desire to know the thoughts of his citizenry; he knew it was for the best that every man and woman was their own island, here on the island (Ted smiled), but occasionally he wished that he understood Delilah just a little.

She was looking at him as he thought this, face to face, as she settled in closer and closer on her right side to study him. His damp skin seemed to reach for hers like leaves sticky with sap until, finally, they were pressed comfortably together. Her large, black-fringed eyes – there was a black ring around the brown iris, giving them a depth that helped Ted to understand the hackneyed phrase 'drowning in her eyes' for the first time – were locked on his. The rough fingertips of her left hand stroked his clavicle before circling down his chest and back up to rub the tender spot behind his ear. Her eyes never left his and her fingers moved in an attempt to soothe him. It was having the opposite effect. He had absolutely no idea what she was thinking. He wouldn't even attempt a guess.

'Death by Delilah,' he said again, shifting in arousal.

She smiled, lowered her eyes and leaned in. He thought she meant to kiss him. At the last moment she swooped lower and bit him at the bottom of his neck. It was not a love bite; she sank her teeth in hard enough that he carried the red mark for the rest of the day. Looking close enough, anyone could see the imprint of her crooked front teeth; he proudly left an extra button undone on his shirt (it was summer after all). The next morning, the red mark was a dark blue half-moon bruise.

Even the bruise made him happy.

Now the bruise was gone, as if it had never existed, and it had been too long since they'd been together (another reason the sheriff had less patience with the tourists' shenanigans). Making his way towards the path to the beach at the end of Delilah's driveway, Ted remembered her latest garden improvement. He paused to regard the newly exposed fence behind the herb garden. He thought of it as his own mark upon her property. His chest puffed out again. Admiring Delilah's obsessive gardening habits, Ted fully expected to see the two little apple trees he'd given her neatly espaliered to the pinky-red cedar. Their trimmed branches would be spread and attached to either wire or strong twine so that the eventual growth would cover the fence in lush, neat waves of green spotted with the occasional delicious Arkansas Black apple. He did not see this. His pause lengthened. His chest deflated.

The apple trees were neatly planted all right. They looked bright and healthy, no sign of shock. Both trees had correct basins of soil around them, drip lines placed carefully under the smooth layer of mulch. But they weren't espaliered; they held their original bushy forms and stood out from the fence a good three feet. Ted felt pulled in multiple directions – he thought they had determined on a plan together. He wanted to ask what had gone wrong, when she'd changed her mind, why she hadn't discussed it again with him; he really wanted to find those tourists and put the fear of the law into them – but the bellow of the arriving tow-truck's horn decided him.

He turned around to meet with the tow-truck driver. The yellow Camaro was loaded to go, and Ted was still dealing with that when a sunburned tourist wearing a stupid hat like Gilligan came tearing down the graveled drive. This gentleman was not the owner of the garage-blocking Camaro, but the driver of the rented Ford station wagon. This was not the type Ted was expecting. Ted felt bad towing the car of a guy who not only had a cranky-looking wife and three puny children, but also terrible taste in hats, so Ted didn't tow his rental car. He did, however, give him a citation with the maximum fine available, and a stern warning about trespassing and vandalism.

The wife – Ted wasn't sure what exactly about her made him uncomfortable, but he recognized 'mean' when he saw it – wanted to protest his allegation.

'Why do you say "vandalism"?' The woman's face was sunburned like the man's, but sourer. She pushed past her husband, the children scattering and then reassembling in the very back of the Ford. The three of them watched the grown-ups from the safety of the open window. Their city-pale, pinched faces reminded Ted of his dead mother's chickens watching from their rickety henhouse, which had finally been taken by a late-winter hurricane – chickens and all. Ted felt sympathy stirring again, and the mean wife must have sensed this, for she relaxed her stance in triumph.

Then Delilah moved. Until the wife got involved, Delilah had seemed content to oversee the proceedings from her porch steps. Ted knew she was there, of course, but was trying to ignore her. Why had she defied him with the trees? She was drinking lemonade, her legs stretched out, feet bare, her elbows hooked on the step behind her. Her hair was still mostly loose but two untied braids in front kept the rest of the curls confined behind her shoulders instead of covering her chest. Delilah wasn't wearing a brassiere under her camisole. Oh yes, Ted was aware she was there. But when the wife walked forward, Delilah put down her glass and walked to her gate. She moved slowly, silently, yet somehow obtrusively. This was not the subtle girl who quietly argued with Maisie Thompson across the counter of the hardware store, respecting her authority and years, even as they both enjoyed their sparring. This Delilah intended to intimidate.

Delilah didn't need to speak; she just leaned against the wooden gatepost. She'd washed her face, neatened that hair, but she still wore the skimpy top and cut-off jeans. Her clothing looked skimpier as she approached. There was no visible reason for her to make anyone nervous. She stood with her weight on one leg, hip thrust out. She rubbed her left hand over her exposed right collarbone and slowly moved her gaze over the wife. The other woman – wind-blown, bedraggled with beach sand and child-rearing – over forty and overweight, flushed even redder than her sunburn.

'Pulling down a chain marked "private property", throwing it in the dirt and driving over it,' Ted said again slowly, looking back and forth between the women. They didn't look back at him, their eyes locked on each other. 'Vandalism and trespassing.'

The wife and Delilah were still eyeing each other in a manner Ted didn't even want to understand. Whatever passed between them – a strange expression like gloating hostility was on Delilah's face – caused the wife to abruptly turn around and climb into the passenger seat of the Ford.

'Let's go, Jimmy,' was all she said.

Jimmy took the ticket from Ted and got behind the wheel. He backed the long car out of the driveway onto Mulberry Street. Jimmy and his wife never met Ted's eyes again, but from the back of the car the smallest child waved bye-bye. Ted waved back before securing the driveway chain.

When he turned around, Delilah was back on the steps. Her glass was empty. She stretched her arms over her head, then snaked them both behind and under her hair to lift it off her shoulders again and drop it with a final sigh of relief. She looked over her almost naked shoulder and smiled at him. She looked pleased with the world; she looked pleased with him. As Ted walked over, he told himself he'd handled this as he would have any trespassing complaint. *Perfectly normal*, he thought. *Just another workday.*

'I have tonight off,' he said, ruining normality.

'It's Friday,' Delilah said. She opened her hands apologetically.

'Have you ever thought—' Ted said. Her eyes flew open as her head pulled back, and she no longer looked pleased with him. It scared him how very far from pleased she looked. When his radio crackled from the cruiser, cutting off his sentence, Delilah was not the only one relieved to hear him be called away.

He had to go be the sheriff, not Ted the man who had trepidations, and he walked to his cruiser. 'Monday,' he called over his shoulder. It wasn't a question, and he couldn't see her face.

'Thank you, Sheriff,' Delilah said loudly in response. When he faced her again in order to enter the cruiser, she waved bye-bye exactly like the departing child.

Ted left to help with the drunk-and-disorderly call on the other side of the island and then two more calls of an urgent nature. The rest of the weekend was even more hectic, as if the tourists were conspiring to keep him so busy he didn't have time to brood over his... whatever Delilah was to him. He hadn't liked that look in Delilah's eyes when he dared to hint at her thoughts on the future. He didn't catch even a glimpse of Delilah again until Monday, and he was relieved, because it gave him time to think. If Delilah had problems of a tourist nature, she handled them herself. By God, he hoped she handled them all by herself. To think otherwise, to think of who might also be handling Delilah's problems – handling Delilah – was more than he could stand until he could see her again on Monday. Question her on Monday. By then he'd forgotten all about the apple trees that she hadn't espaliered. He had more important things on his mind.

A Non-Garden
Apartment

Of course, Alan came back to the Garden. He came back with a picnic that to self-supporting Delilah's eyes seemed a feast. He spread a thick car blanket on the lawn the Garden supplied visitors with for this very purpose – mowed and raked to a velvet smoothness by Delilah – and she had her very first picnic on her lunch hour. Aside from the tendency to attract insects, she thought eating outdoors was very enjoyable indeed; eating food someone else had paid for was outstanding and eating with Alan required little input from her. At the end of the sixty minutes, during which she had listened to Alan talk about his job, his hobbies and the various high-status items he owned, she wiped her mouth delicately, murmured, 'Thank you,' in her most demure voice and disappeared to the back sheds until Alan was gone.

Uncle Martin was sharpening his scythe but paused when Delilah entered, dipped him a grave curtsey worthy of a Southern belle in a ball gown, instead of an assistant groundskeeper in grubby overalls, and then skipped back to the wheelbarrow of composted horse manure that awaited her. She looked just as happy to see the manure as she had when Ronald from Maintenance came to find her to tell her the news that an older man was asking for her. Uncle Martin returned to his whetstone, his judgment reserved. He didn't even shake his head, but he was also careful later not to tell his wife.

*

Alan wasn't there the next day, but he did show up the day after. There was no time for a picnic, but he brought her a sack from the French bakery that no one who worked at the Garden could afford to frequent and a fragrant cup of coffee in a tiny paper cup. He asked Delilah if she were free for dinner Thursday. No mention was made of the odd choice of day: not Friday nor Saturday, but Thursday. Delilah didn't bat an eye – or, well, she did, but in a charming manner that conveyed how thrilled she was to be asked. How very pleased, yet surprised. Yes, truly surprised. How kind that Alan should think of her. How obedient of him to fall gently into her scheme (this last, she didn't share).

She agreed to meet him at the restaurant he named, thanked him sweetly for the gift of sustenance and turned down the path to the large barn. Uncle Martin was glad to accept the snack Delilah offered. He ruled the pastry tasty enough but hardly worth the price. The coffee was too strong and contained skim milk. Delilah patted him consolingly on his bowed head, not hearing a word he said. She wasn't afraid to touch Uncle Martin the way people casually touched their friends – not that she'd had a lot of friends. But Uncle Martin was her friend. Uncle Martin was the first grown man she'd ever spent time with who didn't make her nervous or uncomfortable. She wasn't even on her guard with him. Really, she found him very easy to be with. She thought it had a lot to do with Mrs Martin and the look Uncle Martin got when he spoke of her. It had much to do with that, really – and how he loved gardening. Uncle Martin loved gardening almost as much as Delilah did. How could anyone who loved gardening be bad?

On Thursday Delilah borrowed the third-best dress of her room-mate – a redheaded girl whose name Delilah was almost certain was Annamarie – and received a good-natured lecture from Uncle

Martin's real niece about dating in the big city and what, exactly, a sugar daddy expected of girls. Delilah nodded politely as she remembered Abuela saying *Querer es poder* – 'where there's a will there's a way' – every morning as she applied her red lipstick. She sincerely thanked the girls for their help, and left for dinner with all the gravity befitting a job interview.

Alan was a gentleman. He held her chair, offered to order for her, acted interested in her job and living situation, was genuinely sorrowful over her orphan status, and Delilah never even saw the check for the dinner. Her menu was bare of all prices. Delilah thought that was a neat trick. She drank one small glass of weak white wine and therefore allowed Alan, at the end of the meal, to put her in a taxi he paid off. She'd walked to the restaurant, and her feet ached in the borrowed sandals. Unless she was very much mistaken, she had at least two blisters.

After leaning through the open window to kiss her cheek like an avuncular almost-uncle ('almost', because Uncle Martin had never, not even once, kissed Delilah's cheek and would frown in that fierce way of his had he seen Alan do so), Alan asked to see her Monday. Delilah didn't smile as she nodded in agreement. Of course they would see each other again. Naturally. In what world would they not want to see each other again?

The taxi driver whistled softly between his teeth as he drove her across town. He had two small daughters at home, safely tucked in their beds and years before he needed to worry about them the way that some father somewhere should be worrying about the girl – she looked to be eighteen or nineteen at most – who pulled her shoes off the moment they left that obviously up-to-no-good rich older man in their rearview mirror. The barefoot girl said, 'Thanks,' very softly when they arrived at her building, but she never looked him in the eye. The taxi driver gave his daughters extra-hard hugs the next morning before their mother walked them to school, and he thought of the young girl sitting unprotected in the back seat of his taxi as he did so. His little girls squealed in laughter.

On Tuesday, Delilah borrowed a different dress from another roommate, because the girls were acting a bit oddly after Monday's date. Annamarie expressed her opinion that Alan was probably old enough to be their father, and besides, he looked familiar. Delilah listened as she wrapped gauze around her blistered toes – she was borrowing the sandals again – but Annamarie couldn't place how she knew Alan, just knew in her bones that she did, so Delilah prepared to leave. When Annamarie remembered, Delilah would be grateful to learn what she knew. Annamarie was pleased; people like to be listened to. Delilah understood perfectly.

All the roommates studied Alan, waiting at the curb below, next to his darling little car, as Delilah joined him. He proffered a chaste cheek for her greeting kiss. As Delilah waved goodbye up at the watchers, their red and brown and blonde heads jostling for space at the window looked like the litter of kittens that Delilah's mother had found in a cupboard in the garage and Delilah's father had drowned in the water barrel when he came home from work. Delilah put that memory behind a locked door in her mind. Alan diplomatically pretended not to see his watching jury above, but his delight at Delilah's arrival was not feigned – even Annamarie admitted that.

'Maybe we're being catty,' Uncle Martin's niece, Hannah, said. 'None of us have rich men asking us to dinner.'

'No,' Annamarie replied, as below Alan handed Delilah into the car, ran around to the driver's side and waved at them jovially before driving away. 'No, I know I've seen the old man around. I'm pretty sure he has a daughter our age. It can't be right for him to date someone so much younger.'

'We don't even know her,' the third girl said. 'Not really.' This pronouncement was conclusive and their meeting ended.

The restaurant Alan took her to that night was in a hotel far out of the city proper. It was spacious and private: the staff all but invisible as they served the meal in the dimly lit room, the small tables spaced so far apart that Delilah couldn't tell how many patrons were present, let alone describe them. Alan the avuncular uncle disappeared and a brooding, intense man sat across from her. Delilah wasn't surprised, but she was suspicious.

Pero, ¿por qué? Abuela whispered from her stance behind Delilah's chair. *You knew this was coming, mija. It's part of the dance.*

Alan didn't eat much but kept pushing small bites off his plate into her mouth. Did he feed his children when they were small? A man his age had to have children, right? Didn't rich men marry young, father children to continue their dynasty and then, once they were even richer, jettison the mother of their children? Abuela had said so, then Cousin Gisela's *telenovelas* had cemented the theory.

Delilah wanted to ask him about former wives and current children, but his mood was so obviously sexual, she didn't think she should bring small children into it. She was feeling overly full from the force-feeding and slightly anxious when she waved away the last spoonful of crème brûlée he aimed at her lips. He put it down untasted on the plate under the small bowl. Delilah needed security but she could feed herself, thanks.

'Had enough?' he asked kindly. 'Are you tired?'

'Tired?' Delilah was confused now. Did he intend to take her home?

'If you're too tired for the trip home...' He stopped at the look she felt spreading over her face. Dawning comprehension on top of confusion and condemnation, no doubt.

'Why would I be too tired to go home?' That didn't even make sense. Delilah felt he should work a little harder. Although maybe he was bad at seduction because he'd never done it before? *Maybe he's just lazy*, Abuela sniffed.

Alan looked around and the waiter was almost instantly at his elbow, with the check on a tiny pewter tray. He tried to look apologetic for even offering it, like asking for payment was gauche. 'Perhaps you'd like to charge it to your room instead, sir?'

Delilah felt her entire body flush red as her spine straightened with tension; she was embarrassed now, with the waiter standing next to their table, but her awkwardness could turn to fury depending on Alan's next move. She raised one eyebrow at him. Did he honestly think it would be that easy? He couldn't meet her eyes, but hurriedly threw cash on the waiter's little tray, before standing and pulling back Delilah's chair to urge her out the door. He didn't speak until they were safely folded into his sports car. Delilah relaxed as they drove into the night, away from the insulting hotel. She cracked the window open; here in the country the air smelled like apples, not the sea.

'I thought—' Alan stopped when she convulsively jerked in the seat at the sound of his voice, its tone of aggrieved entitlement. Because of the car, she was forced to sit so close to him that their shoulders touched. 'That is... on our third date... I assumed—'

'I've never done that.' Delilah took pity on his inarticulate bumbling.

'You've never stayed in a hotel with someone before?' He sounded incredulous and she was again suffused with embarrassment, although the anger beginning to creep up her neck gave her the strength to go on. Maybe he thought she no longer had a right to feel insulted – was that what it was? She did not share that view.

'I've never stayed in a hotel,' she said icily. 'And I've never been with a man.'

'You've never been with a man?' Alan sounded horrified now.

'Are you going to repeat everything I say tonight?' Delilah was practically outside her body; she found this conversation so skin-crawling. She searched the darkness around her, trying to find wisdom or *consejo* from Abuela, but now her grandmother was completely silent. Once more, she'd shut the door in her granddaughter's mind, leaving her in all the chaos of her feelings.

'How old are you?' Alan asked and his entire tone changed. Delilah immediately felt like when she'd interviewed at the Garden for a position. Abuela opened up the door to order, *Lie! Always lie about your age. Never give men the truth.* She slammed the door closed again.

'Twenty,' Delilah lied. 'Just.'

'I took a twenty-year-old virgin to a hotel,' Alan muttered to himself and when Delilah heard the quite proper self-recrimination in his voice, she sighed. He possessed common decency after all; she hadn't been completely mistaken in her reading of his character. She shifted a bit deeper into the leather car seat. She'd found her footing again.

'Are you taking me home now?' she asked in her huskiest voice. Alan shifted in *his* seat.

'Yes,' he said. 'I'm taking you home now. But tomorrow' – he coughed – 'if you'll allow me, I'd like to take you out again.'

Delilah was not prepared to forgive him yet – she felt he needed to wriggle a bit more in his suffering.

'I don't know,' she said, looking straight out to the dark road the tiny car traveled. The velocity abruptly slowed as he took his foot off the accelerator at the tremor in her voice. 'You may ask me again tomorrow. For now, I want to go home.'

'Of course,' he said swiftly. 'I'll call...'

Delilah twitched her shoulders.

'I'll come by at lunch, to the Garden. We can talk then,' Alan said. 'I apologize. I never should have...'

He stopped and Delilah held on to what power she had by refusing to speak in reassurance or forgiveness. She was not reassured; her forgiveness had not yet been earned. Alan could afford to dangle from her hook for a night. It would do him good. He was right, after all – he 'never should have' in the first place.

'I want to show you something,' Alan said after he politely escorted her into his car on Wednesday evening. 'An apartment. Not to stay the night!' he added quickly when her shoulders tensed again.

'Whose apartment?' she asked. Her voice deepened even further with suspicion.

'Yours,' he said. And he straightened next to her. He seemed to find speaking easier when sitting next to her in the car rather than across from her at a restaurant table. She supposed some conversations were easier when not face to face. 'If you want it, the apartment is yours.'

She did want it – she didn't even need to see it to know that – but she knew what Alan wanted in return. Delilah told him she would not give it to him, would not *allow* him that, until her name was also on the lease. She was a twenty-year-old virgin all alone in the world, she told him. She had to protect herself to the best of her abilities.

'You're not alone anymore,' Alan said.

Delilah wanted to believe him, she did. But she remembered the Violet Lady's daughter-in-law, Ethel, and how Ethel had to walk backwards after the birth of her baby, and her husband still wouldn't leave her alone. Delilah made sure Abuela's door in her mind was closed and locked, and then she told Alan about her fears. He was happy to discuss them, pleased to hear that she didn't want to be an Ethel. Alan had taken steps, he told her. She didn't have to worry about babies, ever.

Alan found this conversation, Delilah's fear and hesitations, and his place in reassuring her, so arousing that they had trouble walking to the door of the apartment. Alan had to let go of the hold he had on her bottom to unlock the thick oak door.

Looking around was difficult when he wouldn't stop kissing her. She thought there were skylights, but couldn't tell with his tongue in her mouth. Delilah allowed him more liberties than on their previous dates, before reminding him that her name wasn't on the lease and she didn't yet live in the barely furnished apartment that echoed around them. It needed rugs, and she absent-mindedly started a list as Alan continued to kiss her neck, down to the buttons of her blouse. 'Alan,' she said sharply. 'Is it natural gas or propane?'

He stopped attempting to persuade her to visit the bedroom and finished the tour of the kitchen. She kept just close enough for him to touch, but not enough to satisfy him. As Alan drove her home, he promised that the apartment would be hers by the end of the week. Delilah should give her roommates notice and start packing. He'd send movers to fetch her belongings; she wasn't to worry about a thing. And she didn't. She didn't worry about it because the apartment was lovely, and the look in Alan's eye and the stiffness in his trousers said that he was hers, top to bottom, done deal. They shook on it.

She rewarded him by allowing her hand to stray further than it ever had as they kissed goodbye at the curb. She explored areas she'd never encountered before, until Alan held her hair in both his fists, and he had to hold his coat closed when she pulled away and smiled a cheery farewell at him. He rather hobbled around the car to the driver's side. She ran into the building's lobby and never looked back to watch him drive away.

'Did you have a good time?' Hannah, the only girl awake, asked. 'Where did he take you?'

Delilah was not accustomed to the late-night chatter of her roommates; she'd never had friendships at home. Not as a child, not as a girl. She thought Hannah was probably interested whenever the other girls had dates, too, but Delilah's work meant she was physically tired at the end of the day and slept through the post-date discussions of the others.

And Alan was unlike the other girls' dates; he was a grown-up. He was frankly old. Delilah could feel Hannah's judgment like a cold mist rolling in off the sea. She didn't appreciate it; she didn't like the feel of it at all.

Hannah and her roommates no doubt dreamed of marriage and homes of their own and babies, and love with a capital L, but this was not what Delilah dreamed about when she looked at a future, or even future dates, with Alan. Hannah had the comfort of dreaming about love because she was raised in it – she probably did not realize she equated love with security and marriage, and Delilah would never put it into words for her. Delilah was born into a marriage where love did not equal safety, where there was no comfort to be found in respectability. No one had protected Delilah's mother or grandmother, or even her baby self; she knew it was all dangerous. Marriage offered little protection – women were on their own, no matter what. Delilah knew all this, yes, but she wanted a house she could claim. She wanted someone to look at her the way Uncle Martin looked at his wife. She'd been alone for a year now, never fully relaxing for fear of the unknown; she'd try life with the dubious protection offered by a man with money. Hannah was looking at her in expectation or budding worry and Delilah remembered what she'd asked.

'It was a successful date, yes,' Delilah said. She smiled kindly, if tiredly, not hesitant in the least. 'We should talk more tomorrow. Sweet dreams.'

A week later, once Delilah had moved into the apartment that, it turned out, Alan owned – not leased – he told her about his wife, Teresa. He told Delilah about his two children, ages uncertain because he skimmed over them so quickly she never learned their names – children who lived in his house on the other side of the city, on a hill overlooking the sea. Delilah listened without comment, unpacking her clothing from the suitcase and settling her new kitchen to rights. She didn't need to say anything, in truth. She'd known from that first Thursday-night date that there had to be a wife and, from the way he'd put a spoonful of soft custard in her mouth, that he'd fed babies. Men that age weren't unencumbered by family unless they naturally wouldn't be interested in her, or women at all. She'd been raised by Abuela, Lola, once the most beautiful woman in the desert Southwest. And Lola did not believe in mincing the truth. Delilah understood the situation she and Alan were in perfectly well.

Delilah wasn't desperate, she was calculated. Decisions made when desperate were usually unwise. Delilah intended to never be desperate again; she wanted the cushion that money provided. Perhaps she was being naïve, but then she was only... twenty. Yes, she was twenty for now and she could learn her way out of naïvety in Alan's well-appointed luxury apartment just as easily as she could in Hannah's drafty, cramped one. And the bed in which she did her thinking was bigger and more comfortable, too.

The whole apartment Delilah would share with a mostly absent Alan was much warmer and twice the size of the one where she'd shared a bedroom with Annamarie in a room so small it required bunk beds to sleep both girls. Once she quit her job, after Alan suggested a monthly allowance as if it had been his idea, Delilah would busy herself decorating the apartment. Abuela had taught her to sew curtains, reupholster furniture and paint walls. Delilah knew how to make and keep a home. The one for whom she kept it barely mattered; she was mostly keeping herself, after all.

Alan wasn't difficult to please or to keep, it turned out. She thought she might even grow to care for him after a while. He was so desperately happy to see her when he came over – grasping, almost.

It was quite complimentary and gratifying, as long as she didn't think about the fact that what Alan grasped had very little to do with her, Delilah. They'd barely learned anything about one another before he asked her to grace his empty apartment with her presence.

He was always gentle, and he was patient as he taught Delilah what he wanted. As he customized her – that was the way he put it. Mostly he liked just being able to look at her. Whenever and however he wanted. Delilah knew she was a pretty package on the surface, with deep, dangerous layers underneath; that's what Abuela had spent years training her to be. 'Use what you're given, what's available to you.' Abuela wasn't only referring to leftovers or cast-offs.

Alan wanted not *who* Delilah was, but what she *looked* like – that was a given. But he was also a gentleman, with those kind eyes, and he didn't want their arrangement to be even close to blatant. He lived in a rosy-colored play world and Delilah quickly learned his rules to oblige him. *Men make the rules, mija*, Abuela whispered in Delilah's ear. *We make them bend to meet us.*

Delilah didn't ask if 'them' meant the rules or men – she knew they were the same to Abuela. They always had been.

The Iris Walk

On an island overrun by tourists, it became necessary to rise earlier in order to run before the beach was clogged with human detritus carrying cameras and radios and other hazards to a life lived in hiding. Anton started running when the light was still pearly and the world damp. Occasionally, he saw Delilah setting out as he was coming in. Even sleepy-eyed and bed-headed (or maybe especially then) she was so tempting he looked away and mentally whipped up a roux – the least sexy recipe he could think of. But one dawn, he and Delilah finished running at the same time. It was a week after she'd rescued their driveway from predatory tourists.

Because the light lasted so long in the summer – the sunlight lingering in a strange dusk for hours, it seemed – when Anton had returned home that evening after his monthly supply run, he could see that the gravel was churned and furrowed in the driveway, and the little metal sign hanging crookedly on its chain was pockmarked and dinged. If the sign hadn't again been hanging where it should be and if his marshal hadn't told him there was no news on his case, and thus nothing to currently worry about, he would have backed the car out of the mouth of the driveway and driven off the island. Well, that was a lie, he realized, as his car continued to idle there, its driver frozen. He realized he couldn't leave without seeing Delilah again; without one last conversation. And with that recognition, he leaped from the car to unhook the chain. He couldn't leave her and he needed to know what had happened in his absence. He needed to know that his neighbor was safe. No, he needed to know that *Delilah* was safe.

He put his (not his) car in the garage and was standing in the gloom, trying to read the story written in the wildly disrupted gravel of the driveway, when he saw that Delilah was standing outside, too. She was further up the drive, next to her back porch, but there was light in the upstairs of her cottage and music playing. She was waving Anton closer, beckoning to him, with the boyfriend in the house. Anton knew his marshal would want him to turn around and use the front door of the yellow house or leap in the car and take the last ferry back to the mainland and safety. But safety at what price?

Safety from familiarity and involvement and beckoning gestures from a beautiful neighbor he'd found seductive even before she'd laughed at his rude jokes or given him chard or spoken to him with that cat's-tongue voice. Now she was standing in the shadows of approaching dark with her rich boyfriend overhead listening to *Don Giovanni* (what a poser) and she was enticing Anton towards her. He should run the other way.

He walked briskly, purposefully, to her across the disturbed driveway. Delilah took hold of his sleeve with her long, strong fingers and pulled him closer. He dropped his groceries, his grip gone, in order to place one hand on her back; the other covered hers.

'You were right,' she whispered into his ear, that husky voice all chocolate and single-malt whiskey, and Anton knew he'd been waiting his entire life for her to tell him this. 'They are locusts.'

Oh, tourists. His heart left his mouth and settled in his chest once more. Of course, it was those idiots. She had met the tourists and realized they were the enemy. But she was standing so close. Anton's heart beat quicker even as it stayed where it belonged.

'They broke in when I was at the hardware store.' She was still whispering. The skin of her lips tickled his ear. 'I called the sheriff, and had one car towed and another ticketed.'

She leaned back in order to see his face, await a response, but at the same time she released her grip on his short sleeve, and slid her hand down his bicep and forearm to take his hand. He wasn't able to speak. He understood she'd probably lost her balance in the gravel and needed assistance in the dark or, being so goofy, didn't realize she was touching him. Or what that intimate touch would do to him. She, sweet-scented from her bath, and he, who hadn't been touched in any but the most casual way – hello, nice to meet you, here's your change or your dry cleaning – in over two years. When he felt the rough skin of her palm, as sandpapery as her cat's-tongue voice, he was rendered mute by desire.

She didn't mind, or maybe she didn't notice, because she kept speaking even as his fingers clutched hers and his palm pressed closer. His other hand, the one that had reflexively dropped the woven basket of groceries when she touched him, moved from her lower back to cover the back and wrist of her other hand. They stood, sinking in gravel, ankle-deep in spilled groceries, all hands touching, and his head dipped low to hear her soft words. The bats were dark ellipses overhead.

'The woman tried to argue about vandalism, but the driveway sign is bent, and luckily Ted was aggravated because I didn't espalier the apple trees he gave me.' She gestured with her head towards the back garden. 'Remember?'

Inside, *Don Giovanni* stopped bellowing and Delilah jerked in reaction to the sudden silence. Anton tightened his grip on her hands, not just to steady her in the gravel. He was afraid she would pull away. He didn't think he could let go. Not yet.

'Anyway, that's why the driveway is a mess. I didn't want you to worry. Goodnight.' She pulled her hands from his and darted away (her injury must have been healing nicely), but before she left him standing in the now full dark, between 'worry' and 'goodnight', she stood on tiptoe and kissed his cheek. It wasn't a feathery caress, the type that later he could posit he'd only imagined; it was a loud smack. It was the kind of kiss that comic books displayed with a 'mwah' sound bubble, when a heroine bestowed it on her brother or father or a small street urchin. It was the type of kiss, Anton felt, that was worse than no kiss at all.

It distracted him so that he only knew Delilah was gone when the screen door softly shut behind her and the kitchen light was extinguished, leaving Anton to find his groceries and bag them by feel, before blindly walking to his deck stairs more from memory than any physical sense. Anton was left with the belief that Delilah had known exactly what she was doing with that parting kiss, and that led to other beliefs and thoughts, the kind of thoughts that kept him awake at night.

Thoughts about Delilah and the boyfriend; Delilah and Anton; Delilah and the tourists; Delilah and the smacking kiss; and Delilah and the sheriff. For no discernable reason, that was where Anton drew the line. He couldn't think about Delilah and the sheriff. He wouldn't.

The sheriff was someone Anton was not going to think about ever again. Although he had to admit to himself – not to Delilah; to her, Anton admitted nothing, because speaking with her after the hand-holding and the kiss and the running of her scratchy palm down his entire arm was nothing but dangerous – that the sheriff didn't bother him the way horrible Alan bothered him. Anton's current favorite fantasy (okay, second favorite) involved Alan's head and a cafeteria-sized vat of hot marinara sauce – but Anton appreciated the sheriff and Delilah dealing with those locusts. If Delilah had to be with someone who wasn't Anton, better the someone be the sheriff than Alan. But why couldn't she be with

Anton? He inhaled his disappointment, exhaled honest anguish and then went back to finish unloading his groceries. He knew very well why Delilah couldn't be with him.

So the week after, that dawn when he spied her finishing her run, he smiled at her. He smiled a wide friendly smile. He appreciated her; *they were friends*, or at least trying to be. She didn't need to know he had ever wanted to be more than that. He had to be sensible, life-saving, after all. They were neighbors who helped each other out, that was all. *Be serious, man*, Anton told himself, and he gave her the smile you give to pals.

And she followed him home.

Delilah found a photograph in one of Ted's coffee-table gardening books she'd taken while browsing through his shelves to cool off, drinking a glass of room-temperature tap water, after watering his garden. Ted was off being the sheriff, but she knew he liked it when she left him vegetables, freshly picked to keep the plants producing, and little notes telling him what she'd done in the garden that day. Once she left him a slice of Anton's cheesecake, but it felt inappropriate after Ted praised her baking ability and she didn't tell him the origins of the sweet creamy treat. Lying to Ted gave her a sick feeling in the pit of her belly. Oddly, she had no problems with keeping Alan fully in the dark. Alan was happiest in the dark, felt safest there; the dark was his natural home, like a mushroom.

After finishing the chores in Ted's garden and downing her glass of water, she usually made a cup of tea and explored his house. She didn't know if Ted liked that she went through his belongings when he wasn't home, but she doubted he'd deny her the pleasure. Lately, Ted couldn't deny her anything, and the look in his eyes made Delilah worry a bit. She worried that the softening she saw on his face when he stared at her held foreboding. So either Delilah visited when Ted was out cruising the island in his official capacity or, when they were together, she kept him so busy he had no time to stare at her in that soppy loving manner. It made her uncomfortable. The fact that Ted's loving look when he watched her cut eggplants for lunch bothered her, whereas Alan not seeing her even during their most intimate moments did not – well, that wasn't something Delilah wanted to think about. Not ever.

Ted didn't make her uncomfortable in a bad way – she could grow used to a man looking at her with open adoration. Who wouldn't? But he was *the sheriff*, in a small community that thought they knew everything – and what they didn't know they'd make up. No doubt to her detriment.

When Delilah thought about the way Ted looked at her, and knew he wanted more from her, she worried that moving to another small town – on an island, for Pete's sake – perhaps hadn't been such a bright idea. She was both fond of Ted and not ready to give up what she'd achieved, so she didn't think about his wants and needs. Not yet. Maybe not ever.

But she needed to borrow Ted's gardening book. She'd found her next project.

She borrowed the book, even though it made her bicycle lopsided with its unwieldly weight, listing her decrepit raffia basket to one side the entire ride home. Her garden was nearing completion, her men were causing her worry and she needed inspiration. The photograph inspired her. Ted denied her nothing. Therefore, she took the book. Once home, bicycle put away, she poured a glass of sumac lemonade, sat on her new porch swing and prepared to be further inspired.

The photograph of purple fields made her eyes widen, no matter how often she flipped open the marked page to gaze at it. The photograph had been taken at a lavender farm in France and was so gorgeous – purple fields and little stone walls and olive trees – that Delilah wanted to weep in jealousy. She wanted to climb into the book. She wanted to escape to fields of purple. She didn't even like lavender, or at least the smell of it – it gave her a headache and made the back of her mouth taste like soap – but Delilah wanted a field of beautiful purple. Anything purple. Anything except smelly lavender.

She turned a few pages and there was a close-up of a blooming iris, such a deep rich purple that Delilah's eyes ached in their sockets. Delilah developed a plan. She couldn't have an entire field of purple and she didn't want lavender, but she could line her driveway with purple iris and it would be stunning. It would be a column of rich color all the way to where the seagrass started, and it wouldn't leave a nasty lavender-soap taste in her mouth or smell like someone's great-aunt. Delilah reached into the basket next to the porch swing that contained all the catalogues and horticulture magazines she'd taken from Ted's house. She had to hunt down the perfect purple available in her zone and sized for the space. Good thing Ted had never met a catalogue he hadn't immediately sent away for, and good thing he never threw them away once used.

She paid for express shipping when she ordered the iris; she didn't want to wait any longer than necessary. Lately Delilah felt antsy, anxious. It wasn't just men staring at her, imposing their own needs and desires on her; the anxiety was inside her. She felt like she was waiting, but she didn't know for what. Even 'waiting' wasn't the right word. Delilah felt a craving, like she needed something delicious to eat, but she couldn't decide what that might be. Not sweet, not salty, not that other one she could never remember. It wasn't thirst – she wanted to bite something. It wasn't Alan or Ted; she'd tried that. Biting them didn't satisfy Delilah, but she felt she was closer to the truth.

Delilah was worried that deep down she knew who she wanted to bite. She knew what she was craving, but admitting that would change everything, for everyone. *Admit nothing*, Abuela said.

Deny everything. Delilah wasn't ready to face her own needs or desires yet, so she was going to plant a long, narrow bed of iris so purple it'd make a viewer's eyes ache. Maybe hard work and striving towards beauty would tide Delilah's dissatisfaction over. If only for a while.

On Monday, she tried to explain her new iris project to Ted, but for the first time he wasn't interested in garden plans. Oh, he listened, or at least waited patiently while Delilah spoke from her usual spot at his kitchen table, mint tea warming her hands. Ted was crafting grilled cheese sandwiches at his stove. For the first time, his meticulousness, the intensity he brought to each and every task, irritated Delilah. *It's just a sandwich, Ted.* She didn't say it but shifted in her seat, curled her legs under her.

'It would draw the eye up and out, you see.' Delilah placed spoons and a butter knife on the table to represent her driveway. 'Draw the eye away from the yellow garage across the way – so ugly. You'd only see my column of purple.'

She placed the cut-glass napkin holder so that it became the house on the other side of her driveway, and she stopped talking. She only moved to look up from her reverie when Ted turned from the stove to see why she was silent. He placed her plated lunch on her model vegetable garden, over lace placemats that his late wife had dyed lime green, and the utensil driveway disintegrated as Delilah used the knife to cut her sandwich and Ted stirred his coffee with a spoon. He was looking at her again in that way; she felt his gaze on her skin but was careful not to look up into his eyes. She could still feel it, though.

'You have options,' Ted said. Delilah froze with her knife in the air. She carefully put it down on his plate – he needed it to cut his sandwich. It nestled on the ridged edge of the green Fiestaware.

'Like lavender?' Delilah got up and removed the ketchup from the refrigerator. She wouldn't be still when he was looking at her that way. 'Yucky, no thank you. And butterfly bushes are too big. It has to be purple *and* small enough to step over.'

'Not the garden,' Ted said. He took a bite of his sandwich and talked around it. She recognized he was nervous, too, forgetting his table manners. This recognition calmed her – she had the upper hand still. 'I'm not talking about plants.'

Delilah stopped dipping her grilled cheese into the puddle of ketchup on her plate. She glanced up, wary of the look that was waiting for her, and then back down. Nope, she wasn't prepared to hold that gaze. It was too loving, too serious, too intense. That gaze held intentions, and the intent was to complicate her situation, make demands. Ted wanted more. She quickly bit off the red-coated corner of her sandwich, before it could drip, and chewed it neatly.

'You have other options,' Ted repeated. 'If you want—'

'Well, I am,' Delilah said. She was staring at the napkins in the cut-glass holder. It held the gleam of yellow like Anton's house on the other side of her driveway. Ted handed her a napkin. She turned the paper square over and over before placing it next to her plate, unused. She didn't look up. She had the power. The power of not caring as deeply. She could hurt him much worse than he her. This should make her sad. It should, but it didn't, so she didn't examine the strength she felt as she sat straighter in her chair. 'I am talking about the garden.'

It was Ted's turn to be wary. He'd never heard that tone from her – so firm, so assertive. She was talking about the garden, the tone implied, and only the garden. She picked the napkin up and meticulously wiped her hands, scrubbing the nail bed and between each finger. She frowned with concentration.

'All right,' Ted said, and he stopped eating. 'All right, tell me again about the lavender.'

'*Not* lavender,' she responded instantly. She sat properly in her chair to put her bare feet on the linoleum. 'Anything but lavender. I ordered iris.'

She smiled at him, finally, but there was something in that smile. Was it a little hesitant? No, distant. It was the smile she offered to babies and the elderly. When Mr Thompson greeted her outside the hardware store while Delilah parked her bicycle and didn't know Ted was nearby, watching, Mr Thompson received this smile in return. It was her public smile. It filled the sheriff in him with trepidation – he didn't trust that smile on a professional level. It hit like a con. On a personal level, Ted felt all the hair stand up on the back of his neck, and he rubbed his arms briskly to get rid of the goosebumps that rose to warn him. Delilah used the napkin he'd given her to wipe her mouth, and the smile went away. She placed her hand on his left wrist and soothed up to his elbow, gently scratching. Somehow, even that felt impersonal.

Delilah, hands clean of grilled-cheese grease, flipped open another gardening magazine from the pile of mail on Ted's kitchen table. She needed Ted to stop telling her about options, stop making her offers she'd have to refuse. Why were men born to ruin good things?

In the magazine was a photograph of a tiny stone house next to the ocean. The article was about grasses: tough, sturdy, hardy-growing grasses. Delilah didn't read it. She had no room for grass meadows, and anyway her garden was almost done. The photograph of the house reminded her of the photograph in the real-estate catalogue Alan had brought her over a year ago.

The photograph of her cottage had been cropped so that the shared driveway was not shown; the yellow house looming next door was missing. One mostly saw the gray weathered walls, the white-painted shutters and railed porch, and the picket fence surrounding the autumnal garden. Even through the medium of the blurry catalogue page, Delilah could hear the cottage calling to be saved. It needed to be cleaned and cared for. The garden wanted to be beautiful.

Alan liked the price, the remoteness, the aging community and Delilah's eagerness. In Alan's mind, her eagerness to possess the cottage was leverage. She wasn't unaware of this fact. Delilah knew there were options – she could have told Ted this but didn't. Because what would be the point? She had always understood her options, and the cost of each one.

Alan was the price Delilah paid for her cottage, her garden, her accounts at the grocery and hardware stores. Alan was the price she was willing to pay; she'd been willing to pay. Now, almost a year later, she didn't want Ted complicating things with his own brand of options. She didn't want Ted to be the price she paid. She didn't want to think of him like that. She didn't want to think about her cost of living. She didn't want to think about what she'd owe him if he loved her.

It was so much better, much more beautiful, more tranquil, *easier*, to think about a line of purple iris leading the viewer off, away from the cottage and the garden and the cost of all that Delilah paid – one way or another. Better to think about beauty.

In her enthusiasm to quench her craving for beauty, she bought too many of the iris. After two days of dawn-to-dusk work on her knees, digging a trench, adding bonemeal and iris rhizomes, and filling the trench in again, she still had iris to spare. She stood slowly, her joints creaking and popping like her old doll's legs, and she found herself facing the yellow house.

The yellow house had nothing like a garden. In the front grew that lone blue spruce, a misshapen monster that shaded the garage and the front of Anton's house, but that was it. No flowers, no shrubs, not even a scrawny willow or some saw-edged seagrass softened the barrenness of the yellow house's exterior. The gravel of the drive went all the way to the yellow skirting of the house, but surely, Delilah thought, there was enough soil for a line of iris rhizomes? All she would have to do was spade the gravel back, dig another trench, shove the soil and gravel back in, and voila! The purple would look startling against the bitter yellow wall. Anton wouldn't even have to know.

But no. Delilah realized that wouldn't be honest of her. Besides, even Anton would notice the flowers when they appeared. He was so territorial; he might be angry she'd gone onto his side of the driveway. He might consider her a locust, too. She'd better talk to him about the joys of purple iris lining both sides of the driveway, the beauty of symmetry. She'd ask him tomorrow after their run. Until then, she placed the waiting iris in her garage, on the soil floor under the workbench, with its dusty shelves containing items best forgotten. Rhizomes should always be stored in cool darkness. Delilah was one who liked everything, and everyone, in their proper place.

Anton said no. Delilah followed him down the beach path onto his deck. He'd smiled at her after their run, a wide, sweet smile. He'd looked delighted to see her – so happy, she thought he'd be thrilled for her to follow him. Maybe he'd feed her breakfast. Anton knew about cooking, about food. Maybe he could solve her weird craving. Maybe he'd give her something to bite.

But then he looked worried on the deck. He no longer smiled as he had on the beach. Even though she'd kicked her shoes off like he had, he still squinted in anxiety when he looked at her. He let her into the kitchen, though, and offered her a glass of water. She refused, even though she was thirsty. Anton listened politely enough to the iris-walk idea. Or he acted like he was listening.

'Just one side of the driveway will look lopsided, see?' Delilah drew a line with one finger on his floury countertop. Then she added a second parallel line. 'But two lines of purple iris? Spectacular.'

Anton drank more water, quickly, before refilling his glass at the tap, standing sideways-on to her so that he never showed her his back. Did it make him nervous to have her in his house? She took the water glass from his hand, and sipped to wet her mouth and dry throat, before handing it back in order to elaborate on the diagram of the driveway, their shared driveway, dragging her finger through the silky white powder. Once she added Mulberry Street and wavy lines for the ocean, disturbing Anton as much as the flour that covered the counter if his avid stare was anything to go by, she took the glass of water from his hand once more and drank it all down, not ladylike at all. She thirsted. She wiped the back of her hand over her mouth; her mother would not have approved of that gesture either. But Abuela would. Anton hadn't offered her a napkin, not even a paper one. He was watching her every movement, dark eyes tracking her from mouth to floury fingertips, but silently.

'It'll be so easy,' she said. 'I'm only asking for your blessing. I've got it, right?'

'No,' he said. And he shook his head as well.

He said no. Delilah couldn't believe it. Maybe he was so busy watching her that he hadn't listened to her words, her simple yet gracious plan. Again, she explained the beauty of symmetry, the lustrous glow of purple pulling the eye, the ease of trenching and her willingness to do all the labor. Surely, he could see it with her now. But he merely said no again, and offered no further explanation. She stiffened in consternation, scalp tight.

'Why not?' Delilah asked him. 'What's wrong with it? What's wrong with you?'

'I think it would be pointless,' Anton said. 'Just, no.' He cocked his head and waited for her response. But his body suggested eagerness; there was an electric pulse radiating off him. This was not cranky Anton testing her willingness to chain the driveway, abide by his rules. This was an Anton tense with emotion, yes, but not irritable. He was waiting, but he seemed pleased. Did he want her in his house?

In her shock at his obstruction, she could not take her eyes off him. She stared at him so hard that he finally shifted uncomfortably where he stood, leaning against his sink. Anton had obviously baked the evening before and their bare feet were coated with flour kicked up from the floor. Delilah did not think highly of Anton's housekeeping; her floor would have been swept and mopped by now. Her counters would be squeaky clean. What was wrong with him? Delilah continued to stare, and now Anton looked serious. He leaned forward a little, into her personal space. He didn't frown but looked prepared to if, say, she continued arguing about iris instead of... what? What did he want? He had never looked so serious – not at her, not in all their time together as neighbors and as... whatever else she and Anton were. What was he thinking?

She knew what she was thinking, and what she wasn't. She wasn't thinking about rewarding his behavior, his inexplicable behavior (it was inexplicable, wasn't it? Was she fooling herself?), but about picking up one of the skinny loaves of long bread that reposed on the racks above the counter and hitting him over the head with it. She was staring hard into his eyes, and no doubt there was a promise there, but she couldn't believe it promised anything good. Why was he thwarting her? Why wouldn't he agreeably go along with her plans for the driveway? Didn't he realize she only wanted to create beauty?

Delilah's craving to bite was manifesting itself, and maybe that is what Anton read in her eyes. Anton acted. He stepped forward and kissed her. She was not prepared. She pushed him away in immediate reaction and he met her eyes, patient now, waiting. She was shocked by how different this kiss felt, tasted. She drew her lower lip in as Anton watched, so patiently, and then she was ready. She leaned in and he smiled, briefly, before she ended the smile with her lips.

In response, he pressed her up against the counter and kissed her some more. Delilah, forgoing hitting him over the head with a loaf of bread, kissed him back. The iris walk was forgotten, Ted and Alan forgotten; her craving was building and building. She gave his lip a little nip with her crooked eyetooth; this incited a virtual riot of response as he pushed her into the counter with his entire body, straining to climb inside her skin. Delilah stopped longing to create beauty, no longer desiring Anton to give in to her wishes; this here between them was beauty. She was only desire.

Delilah kissed Anton and Anton kissed Delilah until they both stopped for air, and then they stared at each other again. Delilah felt timid for a moment – she was not in control; all her plans had been for naught. It was a bit like drowning. But Anton smiled. Finally, a friendly grin, like he was saying hello, grew slowly and she stopped flailing. Delilah, still looking into his eyes, but no longer able to remember what it was exactly that she had wanted from him, smiled back. She was at peace. All was well.

Anton leaned over and kissed her gently on the forehead, the way one kisses a child being tucked into bed. And that ruined everything. Delilah's life, as it existed, was ruined. She recognized there was no going back to the life that had been. No going back to Alan, no going back to Ted. Once granted the grace of passion *and* tenderness, how could she ever settle for less?

'Further gardening is pointless because I think we should leave,' Anton said. Delilah scuffed her naked feet in the flour and tilted her face up to be kissed again. Anton obliged. 'Do you think we should leave?'

'Actually,' Delilah said. She bit him on the flesh just below the collarbone, right above his heart, in a testing manner, and was satisfied by what she encountered. Her lips smiled against his skin and she didn't bother to lift them from his warmth before she spoke. 'I do. I think we should leave. I've finished my garden.'

'Well, then,' Anton said. He smiled wider, teasingly. His fingertips dug into her hips. 'Naturally, you have no reason to stay.'

Delilah was sad for a moment, thinking of Ted and his 'options', but then Anton, perhaps seeing thoughts of another man on his beloved's face, quickly kissed those thoughts away. The sensation was so new (they were allowed to *kiss each other*; they weren't alone in this weird, lovely, amazing wanting; how would they ever get enough?) that conversation was paused until they slipped on the slick, messy floor, separating and laughing. She didn't want to ever stop kissing him; this was new and intriguing and dangerous. She wanted to know more. She wanted to feel more. Delilah wanted to want what Anton did, and this shocked her; she'd never trusted a man enough to want to know what he was thinking. This, most of all, was a novel approach.

'Where do we go?' she asked, slightly breathless. 'Do you have a place in mind?'

'I have to make a phone call,' Anton said. She slipped again and caught herself by catching him, laughing. Steadying her, his face fell into her neck, and he was able to inhale her scent of salt and vanilla and the tang of earth, as deeply as he once had on her porch, but this time openly as well. He didn't have to hide what she did to him now, and this filled him with triumph. She was his. After having nothing, not even his own name, for so long, Delilah was his. 'But I can make that call later. Eventually. Let's just get off the island first. We can go on a date. We can hit the road, drive 'til we're hungry. We can find a restaurant.'

Anton was so excited at the thought of a real date, in a town large enough for an actual restaurant, without people staring at them or ignoring their existence, that Delilah was infected, too. In a fever they packed his things, and then, understanding that they couldn't possibly separate long enough for her to pack what she needed, Anton entered the cottage for the first time. He sat on the closed lid of the toilet to not miss one moment of Delilah dressing and brushing her hair as she cleaned up for their date – and they continued the conversation that would go on for the rest of their lives together.

Anton explored while Delilah sorted, packed and neatened the house. Lights flipped on and off as he examined rooms, opened cupboards, whistled at the bed she'd rebuilt and painted. (He refused to think of that bastard Alan in the bed. Refused.) When he finished his self-guided tour and complimented her on the open spaciousness of the rooms, the colors and the artistry of her décor, he was touched to see tears in her eyes. It had been a while since anyone had cared for his opinion. Let alone have it mean enough to cause tears.

'I've always imagined showing this place to you,' she said simply. Anton, remembering the restaurant he'd built in his own mind, at first to keep him sane and later to keep him safe from falling in love with his neighbor, nodded in understanding before kissing her some more.

Means of Escape

There was nothing like a garden in Alan's apartment in the city, not a patio or a balcony to grow a tomato plant on. Without the high, slitted skylights in the kitchen and bathroom, Delilah would have lived in darkness. On the narrow sill of the kitchen window – the only window with sufficient sun – Delilah grew tiny pots of oregano, dill and lemon balm, but she knew it would never be enough. Three little windowsill plants would not fill her needs. Delilah's gardening needs had deep roots.

Delilah quit her job at the Garden the second time Alan brought up how tired she was at the end of digging days and complained about the state of her nails. He enjoyed the sandpapery feeling of her calloused palms running down the skin of his bare back, so he graciously never demanded she cream her hands and wear gloves to sleep in – a practice he'd learned from his wife. Alan emphasized the hard manual labor during his persuasion attempts, but Delilah knew the Garden was too close to his office for his comfort. She assured him that she only used the employee entrance on the far side; she never even saw his building, unless she walked to the Garden's main entrance and looked up.

Alan flinched when he heard this, as if worried that an overalled girl with soil-covered hands staring into the salty sky in the general direction of his building would somehow give him away. But Alan's comfort was paramount, she reminded herself with a gentle pinch of his inner thigh. He flinched again, but then she smiled in satisfaction as he reached for her.

Later, she acquiesced as they rested in the rumpled bed, the white curtains blowing in from the open windows to cool them. She'd hand in her resignation and she was sure that Uncle Martin wouldn't mind if she left immediately instead of giving notice, only...

'Only what?' Alan said, lazily enjoying her rough palms on his lower back.

'Maybe I shouldn't leave until I've found another position,' Delilah said. 'Bills, you know.'

'Send them to my office,' he said. He rolled off, unpeeling their bodies to give her a long arm for scratching. 'And I'll deposit money into an account for your incidentals. Why do you think I opened that account?'

Delilah smiled as she thanked him shyly; she knew he delighted in her shyness, considering their state of undress and current occupation, just as she knew he delighted in the fact that she was a virgin when she met him. She knew she delighted him, and that gave her power, but what she was doing by giving up her job for him worried her. She wasn't just worried about the money or placing herself in his debt; there was a second, strange, wiggling need at the back of her mind. Without the Garden, what was she to do?

Walks in the city's beachfront park didn't satiate her need. Neither did the swift runs she took in the early dawn, dashing through streets empty of people and cars, the world still wet with fog, the day was so new. Visiting the country house with Alan on the occasional weekend when he could get away, and he knew for certain Teresa wouldn't pop in, was worse than useless. It broke her heart.

So much garden, so much space, and two gardeners overseeing it all – Delilah could look but not touch. She couldn't converse with the gardeners, engage in shop talk, because she wasn't supposed to be there; she was to be invisible to the gardeners, the maids, the woman who did the cooking and kept the house. Invisibility would be better, Delilah thought after the second weekend, than the way these people looked at her when Alan wasn't standing right next to her. Or sometimes when he was; he pretended not to see it, so as to preserve everyone's comfort. Chiefly his own.

The country house was no balm and Delilah's wiggling feeling grew worse. Her needs were not satisfied. She threw herself into redecorating the apartment, ending country house visits with the excuse of being too busy, but this was merely a stopgap measure, as there was only so much painting, sanding, upholstering and curtain sewing she could do inside 1000 square feet. She made it work for two years, until she was actually twenty. Alan gave her a new carpet shampooer for her birthday; he believed she was twenty-two.

When she finished the apartment and became truly restless, Alan realized a restless Delilah was a dangerous mistress and that Monday he arrived with real-estate catalogues. After two years there was no reason she needed to be in the city; he didn't need her close at hand every moment. He was secure in her affections and his lust for his new... relationship; that passion had banked to reasonable levels. Alan trusted her. Delilah eagerly joined him in studying the thick, glossy brochures, which smelled of fresh ink and money. She weighed her options.

'This is two towns over,' Alan said from his position in his favorite overstuffed armchair. Its slick leather meant that Alan sat on his spine, his long legs stretched out and braced to prevent him sliding onto the floor. As Delilah stepped between his legs to see the page he held open, she made a mental note to leave that chair behind. Ugly and uncomfortable – who would buy something like that? He'd asked her to leave it alone during her renovations, so she held suspicions about its origins.

'Hmm.' She nodded at the house that Alan, looking hopeful, was pointing to. 'Far enough away, but that's a lot of house for two people. Looks expensive to heat, too.'

At 'expensive', Alan's nose almost touched the glossy paper as he eyed the photograph that had been bold enough to betray him. 'Yes,' he agreed, hastily turning the page. 'Drafty.'

He dropped the brochure as Delilah sank to her knees between his. He let out a happy sigh as he snuggled deeper into the chair, but this was quickly cut off when she reached to his side to pull out another, smaller, brochure. He heaved a second, this time aggrieved, sigh when she plunked onto her bottom and gave her total attention to the booklet.

'We haven't looked at this one,' she said. She generously ignored his put-upon breathing. 'Cottages!'

'That's the island,' Alan said. He switched to running his fingers through her hair; she only winced when he hit a tangle. 'I didn't think...'

'An island!' Delilah flipped faster through the thin booklet. 'Cottages on an island. I've never been on an island. I've never seen an island.'

Now Alan wound chunks of the thick black hair around his wrist, inadvertently jerking her head back when she froze. She grabbed the roots of her hair to counter the pulling and the pain, but didn't take her eyes off the picture. Alan leaned over her shoulder to see where she was pointing. He kissed below her ear.

'There,' she said. She held the booklet open with her left hand and pointed with her right index finger rigid. 'That one.'

'Maybe,' Alan said, studying the small photograph. It was black and white, but the listing price was suspiciously reasonable for oceanfront, island property. He needed to put his business brain on and find out what the catch was, and right now he wasn't in the mood, as all evidence indicated. 'Let's think about it and...'

Delilah turned to face him, coming up onto her knees again. She bit her way up his inner thigh. 'This one,' she said when she reached the terminus. 'This cottage. No thinking.'

She pushed him back into the chair, resting her chest on his lower body as she grabbed the telephone on the table at his elbow. Her blouse was gaping open from the strain of their positions. Delilah dialed the number listed next to the cottage on the island and handed the receiver to Alan. As they waited for the number to click through and the ringing to begin, Delilah made another trip across Alan's body, this time slowly, gently biting her way down his chest. Soon his clothing was as disheveled as Delilah's. By the end of the telephone conversation, Alan was having trouble concentrating and the realtor he spoke to believed him to be an elderly asthmatic. By the end of the month, Alan and Delilah owned a cottage on an island that neither of them had ever seen.

The Last Ferry

The ferry was late. Alan was forced to sit in line, waiting, sucking in the exhaust from cars whose owners didn't have the decency to cut their engines. This, after he'd left the city and his house early, thinking he'd surprise Delilah with a morning arrival. He chose to ignore the well-known fact that she didn't like surprises; she found surprises threatening. He chose to imagine her delighted at seeing him hours and days ahead of schedule, her crooked smile of joy and her arms around his neck in a warm embrace of welcome. That their impromptu trip to the mainland on his whim that one night had been an awkward, almost hostile, disaster was surely a one-off; Delilah hadn't felt herself that night. Nor the next morning. But today would be different: maybe they'd take a walk on the beach, enjoy the roar of the waves, discuss the new direction their life together was about to take. Alan stretched to the best of his ability while cramped up in the too-small car, and told himself he was stretching in anticipation.

More cars lined up behind him. He eyed them in smugness in his rear-view mirror. They should have had the foresight to arrive early, as he had. But the ferry was late because the end-of-summer tourists were unruly and the ferry captain couldn't maintain enough order to depart the island, unload the sunburned rabble and ready the vessel for the return trip in a timely manner. Alan felt that the captain should run a tighter ship. He smiled at his own joke.

The line of cars on the causeway finally began to move and Alan had no further room for reflection until his Porsche was stowed safely. He had a paper cup of tepid coffee in his hand, and a seat out of the spray but with enough breeze to keep comfortable. Alan didn't like to sweat and he had a lot to think about. There were decisions to be made – plans needed forming and steps taking. Alan was accustomed to all that; he welcomed the mind-work of it. But he didn't like ultimatums, and he had been given one.

Teresa, after thirty years of marriage and two kids and two houses (that she knew about) and three cars and that stupid horse that no one ever rode, had given Alan an ultimatum. Teresa, it turned out, knew about Delilah. She'd known about her all along. She knew about the apartment where Alan had kept her. More importantly – in Teresa's exact words – now she knew about the cottage he had bought for Delilah. Her brother Louis had done a little digging; he'd never trusted Alan. And Alan had only himself to blame for acting so guilty when Louis innocently bumped into him that afternoon outside his love nest. The apartment was one thing. However, Teresa wasn't going to stand for a beach cottage in another woman's name. The situation would not do.

On the top deck of the ferry, in the cooling breeze with a sea spray that only mildly reeked of diesel, Alan's scalp tightened in remembered anxiety. Teresa was willing to put up with a lot; she'd known about Delilah, known about the apartment where Alan paid the mortgage, and she'd said nothing. *Why* she'd said nothing made him actively uncomfortable.

'Maybe you're having a midlife crisis,' Teresa had said to him the night before. 'Maybe you needed a fling to settle your nerves or feel like a man again.'

Alan flinched at the memory and crossed his legs.

'But buying this girl, young enough to be your daughter, a beachfront cottage?' Teresa's rage steadily increased. 'Taking the food from your children's mouths in order to *feather your love nest*? That I will not tolerate. You will settle this. Or I will.'

Their son was in law school and their daughter was engaged to a lawyer, so Alan didn't think either of them was in danger of losing any meals, but Teresa had that look in her eye that Alan recognized as a warning not to disregard her motherly feelings and he didn't backtalk. He listened quietly to his wife's ultimatum and then slept in the guest room the rest of the night. At dawn, he'd dressed, walked to the garage where he kept the Porsche and hit the road. Being stymied by the late ferry was unfortunate, but it gave him time to mull. Not that he truly needed it; Alan knew what had to be done, after all.

Two children ran from their parents, who called after them, 'Stay close!' and 'No running!' It was a little girl chased by a smaller boy, reveling in the freedom of escape from the car; neither child paid a lick of attention to the parental instructions. Right at Alan's feet, the girl hit the deck (Alan almost smiled at his own pun again), spilling jujubes and skinning her knees on the wet sandpapery texture of the ferry's flooring. She didn't cry but sat, stunned. The little boy stopped, too. He walked sedately back to crouch and study the bloody, abraded skin of her knees, scarlet blood welling up to bead here and there, the exact color of the spilled hard candy. Alan offered his clean handkerchief. The girl accepted it with a shy, 'Thanks, mister.' Together, Alan and the boy kicked the spilled candy off the side of the boat to avoid further mishaps. Leaning on her little brother, the child limped away. Alan's handkerchief was tied sloppily around the knee which bore the worst injury.

She'd reminded Alan of Delilah, with her messy dark hair and her suffering in silence. Delilah's silence was one of Alan's favorite things. She didn't even hum when she thought herself alone. When he'd first met her – she was working in the botanical garden where he walked at lunch – he'd thought she might be mute. But no, she was silent by nature. She was one of those people who preferred action to words, quick decision to rumination. Alan wondered what action she'd take when he told her his news. He threw his empty cup in the trash and sat down again. The bench was damp from the spray, but he'd given his handkerchief away so he'd just have to deal with a wet ass. Teresa would say he was risking piles.

Teresa was a talker. Teresa believed every possible option should be discussed – no, analyzed – before decisions were made and outcomes revealed. Last night, Teresa had told Alan he could lose Delilah, sell the house and the apartment – lose all that – or he could lose his family. Teresa made it very clear and then she stopped talking. That's when Alan knew she was serious. A quiet Teresa was a scary Teresa.

Now, Alan needed to make a decision, and he had until he reached Delilah to do it. Did he want to give up Delilah? Did he want to give up the power he felt with her? Delilah would never give him an ultimatum as Teresa had. But did that mean he should give up Teresa for her? Did he want to give up the familiarity, the security of his marriage? There was a certain comfort in knowing what to expect. Even if part of that knowing was his wife's ultimatum when he broke the rules. And he knew she meant it, but he wasn't sure if Teresa was prepared to face the unknown either. The unknown outside of the secure world they'd built in their marriage, broken vows and all.

His children were grown and he thought Teresa had raised them to be reasonable people – surely he wouldn't lose them? If he gave up Delilah to keep Teresa, would Teresa forgive him? And forget his trespass against her? She'd forgiven him in the past, but he'd never bought anyone a beach cottage in the past. He wasn't sure Teresa could ever forgive him a trespass on the scale of real estate. Some things just couldn't be forgiven.

*

There was a flutter, a bird's unfamiliar cry, and Alan awoke from a sleep he didn't know he'd slipped into. It was full daylight and the windows of Delilah's cottage were open, the white curtains moving in a breeze that smelled like salt water and something herby. Rosemary? There was a bird, a small tawny thing, clinging to the screen with its claws. Its wings were beating against the net to maintain balance and it was this noise that Alan heard like a foreign heartbeat.

He was not in the bedroom. He'd fallen asleep on the uncomfortable, minimally padded wooden divan in the living room of the cottage he'd bought for Delilah, thinking his wife would never know. The walls, floors and ceiling were all painted a pearly white, and what little furniture the room contained was either plain sanded wood or painted in pastel colors. In consequence, the room reflected so much light that Alan couldn't believe he'd fallen asleep – let alone deep enough to dream.

He couldn't remember the dream, only the feeling of it. Some kind of loss, or he was alone and in danger. He was in a stark emptiness filled with light that hurt his eyes. He'd misplaced something or he'd been misplaced. He wasn't even looking for it, whatever it was, in the dream. He was mourning what was lost. This dream possessed the subtlety of a hammer.

The rosemary scent intensified with the wind. The sun must be shining on the bush covered with purple blossoms that grew outside the window and all along the porch steps. Alan had brushed up against it when he'd entered the house that morning. Kicked it as he'd stood talking to the sheriff. The door of the cottage had been unlocked, waiting for him. Maybe the smell was on him, not coming in through the window? Maybe both. Concentrating on the scent meant that Alan didn't have to think about the folded white paper behind the green glass oil lantern on the fireplace mantel.

When Alan stopped thinking about the rosemary lingering on his jeans, he'd have to get up, read the note and think about what it said. He'd have to read what Delilah wanted to tell him. He'd have to know what she'd done, where she'd gone and with whom. Quite frankly, Alan didn't want to know. Not any of it.

But that sheriff wanted to know. If he'd followed Alan into the house the way he'd obviously wanted to, the note would be opened and read by now. Alan wouldn't allow that. Alan refused to read what was undoubtedly a 'Dear John' letter with another man watching. Especially not this man. Sheriff Ted. Alan knew he wasn't the most perceptive man, nor the most observant – Teresa told him this at least once a week – but Sheriff Ted wasn't hiding his personal interest in Delilah's whereabouts and well-being. Alan suspected he'd been had. But by whom and to what extent, Alan was still discovering. He wasn't entirely sure he wanted to know everything.

Alan thought back over the times this summer when Delilah hadn't answered the telephone or had seemed reticent about her habits, actions or plans. Alan, appreciating her silence, her discretion, hadn't pried. He'd just gone on living his unperceptive life, thinking of himself, his happiness; living every man's dream. Two women, two households; any half-assed fool would have known that couldn't last. The sheriff seemed to know. When Alan hadn't taken him seriously at first, he'd looked ready to arrest him. Or shoot him. Maybe just slap him silly. Alan, after his mind-clearing nap, didn't blame him.

Delilah was gone. Her closet was empty of everything except the dresses he'd had his secretary pick out for her birthday or Valentine's Day gifts – these were hanging limply or dropped in colorful puddles of silk and lace on the floor, as if she'd disregarded them so completely, she couldn't take the time to pick them up and restore them to their proper places on the padded hangers. Her suitcase and overnight bag were not there – so, she'd packed her raggedy gardening clothes – and the refrigerator was clean. All the garbage had been carried out to the curb.

Sheriff Ted pointed out that the cottage and the yellow house had been sharing a garbage can. This seemed to really upset the sheriff – apparently, it was an island culture no-no. But Sheriff Ted's emotional reaction was exceedingly personal. With that realization, Alan got off the uncomfortable divan and went to read the note left behind the green glass lantern. The scent of rosemary followed him.

'Alan Trier?' the sheriff had asked. His hands were at his sides, not aggressive at all, but his tone was not casual. Even Alan caught the tension in the two words of his name.

'Yes, good to meet you.' Alan extended his hand. The sheriff didn't take it, merely eyed it suspiciously. The ferry was emptying around them. Alan was waiting his turn to drive forward.

'I'm the sheriff here,' the sheriff said, pointing with a thumb over his shoulder at the land beyond the dock. They technically weren't on the island yet. Alan didn't think the sheriff would appreciate him making the distinction. 'We need to talk.'

'Is everything all right?' Alan unclenched his hands from their grip on the steering wheel. He didn't want to look nervous.

'We need to talk.' The sheriff looked off towards the end of the line of vehicles waiting to disembark. The wind was lifting his hair from his scalp. Alan couldn't tell if the hair was blond or gray, but then the island's inhabitants had never seemed quite real to Alan.

'May I ask what this is about?' Alan inched the car forward; the other man took two steps to stay abreast of the Porsche's open window. The convertible top was down. Alan felt exposed. Normally, that was a good feeling on the island, as he was going home to Delilah. Let the sea wind blow his city worries away. Today, the exposure was rapidly turning negative.

'There are some official questions that need answering—' the sheriff said and he bit off his words. He looked... angry. Inexplicably angry. Alan worried that Teresa was behind this somehow, but then dismissed that as paranoia.

'What questions?' Alan asked. 'About what? Is Delilah okay? Miss Ortiz, I mean.'

Maybe that should have been his first question when speaking to a representative on the island. Or maybe – Alan's paranoia reasserted itself – he shouldn't have mentioned her at all. But what else could this be about? It wasn't even Friday; he'd never been here midweek. Most of the vehicles surrounding him seemed to be service trucks. Except, in the station wagon ahead of him, there were the little girl and boy he'd met earlier. The little boy was asleep, his head slumped corpse-like on his mother's shoulder, his open mouth stained red with jujubes. The little girl waved his bloody borrowed handkerchief goodbye as the line finally moved off the ferry at a brisk pace.

Alan waved back and the sheriff whirled to see at whom. The man's body wilted in disappointment when he saw the child's dwindling wave. She sat on her hands when she caught the sheriff's eye, as if guilty of wrongdoing. Alan started to worry.

'What is this about?' Alan asked, his foot on the brake. 'Where is Delilah?'

The sheriff's arms dropped to his sides and he slapped his left hand against his thigh. 'Meet me at the cottage,' was all he said before he walked off the ferry's deck. His official vehicle was parked illegally nearby.

At the cottage, Alan didn't let him in. He wanted answers, not an interrogation. When Sheriff Ted told him Delilah was gone, the man next door was gone and a federal marshal was asking after them both, Alan's paranoia said to him, *See? I told you.*

'What is Delilah's real name?' Ted asked. He spoke rather loudly over the wind.

'Delilah Artemisia Ortiz,' Alan said. They were standing on the porch. Alan hadn't tried the door yet, and overgrown rosemary branches were beating both of them about the knees from the force of the wind.

'No,' Sheriff Ted said. He shook his head, a long-suffering look on his face. He hooked his thumbs in his utility belt. 'Her real name. What's her real name?'

'What?' Alan asked, while his paranoia said, *Whoa, didn't see that one coming.*

'The marshal looked her up. Or tried to.' Ted looked desperate now, no longer angry. 'There is no Delilah Ortiz. We need to know her real name.'

'Delilah,' Alan repeated. 'Her name is Delilah.'

'You don't know anything either.' Ted was openly disgusted, his mouth actually twisted as if he had tasted something acrid. No one had been as disappointed in Alan since his father died and took his disapproval with him. 'That's it. They're gone.'

'Who's "they"?' Alan, feeling stupid and stymied and agitated, kicked the rosemary bush. Bees shot out of it in alarm. Buzzing in understandable fury, they searched for their assailant. Both men skidded off the porch to end up by the gate, outside on the graveled driveway. For the first time, Alan noticed that in the garden the plants were dusty, wilted, thirsty-looking. How long had she been gone?

'Delilah and the guy next door. Anton, he called himself. The marshal won't tell me his real name.' When he spoke about Delilah, the sheriff wasn't angry. He was frustrated, worried. Alan's paranoia didn't like the man's desperation. Desperate people were dangerous. 'Mrs Oakapple next door on the other side and Mrs Bradshaw down the street saw Delilah get into the car of the guy from the yellow house, and Jack Silva, the dockmaster, loaded them onto the ferry. After that, who knows?'

The sheriff wasn't reading this information from a notebook; he recited it from memory and then ran one hand violently through his gray hair.

'Was there violence?' Alan was worried for Delilah instead of himself now. Maybe there was a legal reason the sheriff was involved. 'Did he force her into the car?'

Sheriff Ted stopped pulling the hair from his scalp and examined Alan. For the first time he looked almost, but not quite, sympathetic. It wasn't sympathy, because there was too much disdain, and definitely no pity, in his eyes. Ted's eyes were narrowed against more than the sun and perpetual wind of the island. He looked like he resented Alan asking that question, his right to ask that. If he wasn't so concerned, Alan would be getting a little testy in return. Who was this man to judge him? *He's the sheriff, remember?* his conscience replied.

'There was kissing,' Ted said. His fists clenched. 'Not violence. He opened the car door and she willingly got in, and every witness reports kissing.'

'What's this to you?' Alan asked. He was not going to address the kissing – after all, he was a married man – but he was definitely testy now. His inner voice yelled, *Are you crazy? The sheriff has a gun!*

But the sheriff didn't get angry. He calmed down and eyed him. The look reminded Alan of the way his accountant looked at him after discussing the housekeeping receipts of two households, two women. The look said, *You think you're getting away with something, but God, you're a dumb schmuck.* Alan didn't want either man's pity or approbation or, let's be honest, their opprobrium, but this man *was* wearing a gun.

'I'm the sheriff on this island,' Ted said wearily. He rubbed his eyes before staring at the yellow house looming above them both.

'When a federal marshal comes looking for someone, it's only polite to involve me.'

'Why would a marshal look for Delilah?' Alan asked. 'And her name *is* Delilah.'

'Not Delilah.' The sheriff was impatient at this point. He wanted away from Alan, and he turned his back on everything the driveway contained. 'The neighbor. The guy in the car. The man kissing her. They are looking for the man from the yellow house.' Ted thumbed over his shoulder at said house – he wouldn't look at it again. Alan looked up at it instead, and Ted sighed before turning back to hand Alan a card.

'You don't know any more than the rest of us,' Ted said. 'I should feel sorry for you. If she contacts you, call that number on the card. I'll get the message.'

Without looking at Alan or the houses again, the sheriff walked away to his car. Alan went inside the unlocked house, checked every room and closet, and then found the note on the mantel. The sight of it caused him to slump onto the nearest piece of furniture and slip into impromptu slumber.

When Alan read the letter, he understood why the sheriff hadn't insisted on searching Delilah's cottage. He'd already done so. He'd read the note; he'd seen the initial *D* signed at the bottom. He'd no doubt discovered that the journal and *Farmer's Almanac* normally kept in her bedside table drawer were missing. For all Alan knew, Sheriff Ted was intimately acquainted with every nook and cranny of the cottage. She hadn't bothered to write them separate goodbye notes, just left off a salutation altogether.

Thanks for everything! I'll miss you. Please water the garden until the house sells, Ted. The keys and legal papers are in the desk drawer, Alan. The gardening books I've borrowed are on the shelf above. Don't worry about me, we'll be fine. All the best! Love, D.

Alan read the note again. He then went outside to the detached garage, where he hadn't bothered to park his car, and looked for the fireproof lockbox that Delilah (or whatever her name was) kept on the lowest, darkest shelf of her cobwebbed potting table. He'd given her the box their first Christmas together (well, the day after Christmas) to replace the shabby cardboard hatbox in which she kept her family photographs, birth certificate and some newspaper clippings he'd never read. Alan remembered Delilah expressing a strange pleasure in the fact that the garage was so far from the cottage. Alan hadn't paid much attention to her pleasure. Maybe he should have.

Alan had never seen the photographs or read the clippings that Delilah kept in the box. Nor had he seen the birth certificate. When he'd found Delilah repairing an old hatbox with black electrical tape, she'd told him it contained the only things belonging to her dead relatives that she had left. She'd accepted the lockbox with gracious thanks that next Christmas and stored it as far as possible from where she slept. He should have asked why.

The box was gone from the garage. Only displaced, sandy dust smeared across the shelf gave evidence that it had ever been there. No doubt this detail would help the sheriff and the marshal. No doubt this was the kind of information the sheriff was asking for, figurative hat in hand. Delilah's origin story. But Alan was damned if he would be the one to give it to them. He refused to help them find Delilah... and she would always be Delilah to Alan.

Alan collected the keys, legal documents and books, and then left to catch the last ferry off the island. He dropped off the books at the sheriff's station – Ted's name was written on the flyleaf of each – with the note tucked inside one of them. The deputy at the counter flipped open the cover of the top book. Alan felt like remonstrating but instead walked away. It wasn't his book. It wasn't his privacy being betrayed; that ship had sailed. Alan couldn't even summon amusement at his metaphor.

'Sheriff left a message for you,' the deputy called out and Alan turned away from the door.

There was a woman sitting huddled next to the pot-bellied stove in the corner; the stove wasn't lit because it was the end of summer and still quite warm, but she was the oldest lady Alan had ever seen upright and was wearing so many layers of clothing that she'd probably reached the age where she was cold all the time. Aside from her, Alan and the deputy were alone. Sitting next to the stove was probably more habit than sense, Alan supposed. He dragged his gaze away from the old lady, whose scarf was printed with red apples, to the deputy who waited for Alan's attention with bovine patience.

'Sheriff said if you stopped in, I should tell you...' The deputy paused as the old lady creaked to her feet. There were cracks and popping coming from under the many layers of cloth. Both men watched until the noise stopped and she was ambulatory.

'What's the message?' Alan prodded. He didn't care if the lady heard. She was approaching the counter where they stood.

'That marshal called and she said she couldn't give us any information,' the deputy said.

Both men were still watching the old lady walk; this let them avoid each other's eyes while awaiting her eventual arrival. The sheriff's station lobby was not large, but she was incredibly slow.

'That's the message?' Alan asked. 'He called to say: "I can't say anything"?'

'Hmpt.' The old lady agreed with Alan. She had finally reached the counter and clung to it for support.

'*She* isn't allowed to share any information,' the deputy went on somewhat anxiously. He apparently felt misjudged. 'But out of professional courtesy, she wanted us to know that we could call off the BOLO.'

'What does that mean?' Alan felt something floating to the surface and he dreaded it.

'Be on the lookout,' the deputy said.

'No,' Alan said. 'I know that. What did that message mean? She can't share any news, but *don't* be on the lookout?'

The deputy finally met Alan's eyes and then froze in place behind the counter. Something in Alan's demeanor rendered poor Deputy Hayes mute. The two men stared at each other in frustrated mutual horror. Alan's vision was blurry. A small gnarled hand, dry and light as an autumn leaf, rested on top of Alan's clenched fist on the counter. He had forgotten about the old lady. He didn't know how that was possible.

'You stop looking for something, dear,' Mrs Oakapple said, 'when you've found it.'

Her sympathy undid Alan completely. He turned and fled the sheriff's station. The bell hanging from the doorknob rang out once in farewell.

The Ferry Leaving
the Island

It wasn't until they'd left the island, standing at the front of the ferry to face their future, not looking behind at what they'd left, that Delilah gave a thought to who she was leaving. She'd written a note – it was common courtesy, after all, to leave a note – but she'd given no thought to how those left behind would feel about her leaving. She hadn't thought about Ted the person.

'Maybe,' she said, halfway turning, but Anton's body behind her prevented her abrupt movement's completion. 'I should have—'

Her sentence wasn't completed either, and it wasn't only because of Anton's kiss – it was the look on his face as he did it. He saw her; he saw Dolores. She'd left her flouncy dresses and make-up behind – those gifts from Alan, requirements of the job that was Alan, were not really her. The clothing she wore now was really her. Her face was bare, and Anton knew her real name. He was the only one who had ever asked.

Whatever he saw in her eyes then made him smile – it was only slightly triumphant – and he kissed her again. But she didn't completely stop thinking about what she was leaving, who she was leaving. Perhaps one day, Delilah thought, she would send postcards back to the island, like the ones she occasionally sent to Cousin Gisela; postcards back to the island from the home she would create with Anton, the home they would share. Perhaps the postcards would be photographs she would take of their life together. She'd packed the Leica Alan gave her for her birthday. She'd send him a postcard, too. He'd always been kind to her, to the best of his ability.

For Ted she imagined a garden scene of their home in Arizona. No, no, too arid – and what kind of restaurant would they have there for Anton? Not to mention it was a little too close to the home state Delilah would never return to. Not the desert Southwest; a garden needed rain. Delilah would send Ted a postcard of her garden in the Pacific Northwest. Redwoods and ferns and mosses would be the underpinning, the bones she would grow her masterpiece upon. She read that hydrangeas grew to epic proportions in Washington state. Ted would be proud of her and her giant blue hydrangeas. Wouldn't he?

What, after all, did she really know of Ted? How did he feel about her? For her? What did she feel for him, after all? Delilah brushed the sea spray off her face as she pondered whether Ted loved her or if she knew him well enough to have fallen in love with him. She remembered how he'd looked at her when she showed him the finished herb garden, the disappointment in his eyes when she hadn't espaliered the apple trees. Maybe that combination, pride in accomplishments and disappointment when one failed to meet expectations, was love. Maybe that was what it was like to have a father. But then she remembered other emotions and sensations Ted had displayed when he looked at her and she stopped that line of thought. If Ted loved her, it wasn't in a fatherly way.

Delilah would never know how a father's love felt, but she could make sure her own children would know. Anton pulled her hair away from her shoulder in order to press his lips to the side of her face, on her pulse fluttering in her temple, and Delilah decided anew she was making the right decision. Others would realize the same – in time. But that was on them. Their needs and worries were no longer her responsibilities. She could let them go.

To Maisie Thompson, her friend and sparring partner, Delilah would send a postcard of all the pretty appliances in her kitchen. A kitchen decorated and maintained by Delilah. She imagined mopping a black-and-white checkered floor as Anton slipped his hands on either side of her jaw in order to lightly kiss her again and again. A kitchen used by Anton to cook the meals eaten by them as a couple, then as a family with their children. Delilah sent a mental postcard of her children to Maisie as well. They looked like Delilah but with Anton's sweet disposition. Although the longer she looked at him – he kissed her as she did so – the more handsome he became. The more he looked at her, in amazement and gratitude, the less impartial she became. She'd never enjoyed losing her judgment more.

Delilah couldn't remember her own mother looking at her like she was the whole universe, but then she couldn't remember much of her mother at all. Delilah vowed that her children would know her. Her children wouldn't need to remember her, because she'd always be there. Delilah's children would have the privilege of taking her for granted. Anton held her tighter, his arms crossed with hers under her breasts, when he felt the deep, shuddering sigh she took along with her vow. Alan had never held her like that; he'd never bothered to read her emotions. He didn't care what she felt.

Perhaps Delilah would send her baby announcements to Alan and Teresa, too. *See what I made!* Perhaps that would be cruel, or more likely they wouldn't care. Delilah wondered if she would spend the rest of her life questioning – when she wasn't raising her family, gardening or helping Anton run his restaurant – whether or not Alan had ever really cared. Maybe she was just another pretty, high-status plaything like his Porsche or the stallion no one knew how to ride or the apartment that had sat empty until Delilah's arrival. Alan had collected Delilah, too, she knew now. Maybe she'd even known at the time; after all, she'd allowed it to happen. Even as young and inexperienced as she'd been, she'd known she was never more than the 'other woman'. Alan hadn't lied, she'd give him that. But he'd never looked at her the way Ted or Anton did – especially the way Anton was looking at her now.

He lifted her entire face to kiss her below her ear, down the jawbone to the corner of her mouth, and all thoughts of anyone other than Anton stopped. When their lips separated, swollen and tender, Delilah looked Anton in the eye and would have said, 'Alan who?' if asked about her former lover. When Anton looked back, she saw in his expression everything she had ever looked for, and not found, in anyone else's. She was enough for him; he wanted nothing more than what she offered. She saw homes, not houses. Station wagons, not sports cars. Partnership, not mentorship. She saw Anton looking at her bare, open face and something like awe came into his eyes. He tucked the messy hair behind her ears, kissed her gently once more and then asked, 'Should we have a snack when we get to the mainland, before we leave?' And Delilah melted.

She sent a postcard to Abuela in heaven, no longer hovering at Delilah's ear whispering *consejo*. Delilah let Abuela go – she was free to rest. To Abuela's spirit, she sent a photograph of Anton looking at her so lovingly, wanting to feed her before taking her away from here. Anton, dirty kitchen and all, was the *novio* Abuela had dreamed of for her granddaughter without ever knowing it. This postcard was signed 'Dolores'.

Before they'd driven out of their shared driveway, when Anton was backing the car from his garage after removing the chain from the posts one last time, Delilah had entered her own garage to reappear with a lockbox she placed at her feet on the floor of the car. 'Treasure?' Anton asked.

'Yes,' Delilah said. She paused. She thought of her mother and Abuela, and of other memories the box contained. 'Maybe. Of a sort. Kiss me for luck.'

He did. They kissed at the mouth of the driveway, before weaving through the village to the ferry landing. They never looked to see if they were being watched; they hardly looked away from each other at all. Once on the ferry, they faced the open sea, not the island. They never looked at the island again. They never looked to see if anyone was looking back.

The Village

The summer ended and a short, intense autumn saw the village residents through what they came to realize was collective shock. Immediately after the disappearance and a round of fact-sharing (it wasn't gossip – they were genuinely concerned for the girl's well-being and the sheriff's sanity, and conjecture wasn't helpful to either), the islanders stopped discussing what happened in those houses, that driveway. What good would discussion do?

Gone was gone, and their sturdy fortitude didn't believe in wishful thinking. Those so inclined spared a few moments to pray for the girl, whatever her name might be. She'd need their prayers, running off with that Mafia type. Alan, they didn't give much thought to – a married man making a fool of himself, and in that silly car, too. Anton's ancient Renault was more the island men's speed, but they never did learn his name. No one thought of Alan after sharing the story of his departure from the sheriff's station. But a few of the women, led by Mrs Oakapple, did throw out a wish or two for his wife. They wished her well, but they also wished for her to give Alan hell.

By fall's end the villagers, starting with the older women, forgave the sheriff what they saw as his temporary insanity. *He was lonely,* the women said. Who could resist her? The men of Ted's generation shrugged. The men of Delilah's age didn't say anything; they were still pretty resentful.

'If I had known she was looking for someone to run off with, I'd have tried to talk to her,' said Ray Ramirez, but then looked over his shoulder in case his wife or mother or the sheriff was nearby. His friends checked, too, but no one laughed. No one wanted to laugh at Ted. And they didn't want him to see their pity. But he wasn't there behind them. Ted was keeping to himself.

Ted was keeping busy preparing his garden for the winter. The dead annuals he cut back, pulled out or mulched over. Any late seeds he saved. The buddleia bushes he cut almost to the ground; they only bloomed on new growth and Ted intended to have a bumper crop of sweet-smelling purple blossoms when the time came. He needed something to look forward to. The deep blue hydrangeas he gave a wide berth. Those were on their own.

The rose bushes, trees and ramblers were trimmed to the point on each branch where leaves of five appeared; later they would be swathed in burlap and loosely tied to prevent the strong Atlantic winds from ripping them away, but it was too soon to cover them now. Ted was starting his clean-up early because, once he finished his own garden, he fully intended to go put Delilah's garden to bed. He didn't care what the marshal said; she'd always be Delilah to Ted.

Heaping a pine-scented mulch over his raised beds, Ted planned his approach at Delilah's. He'd start out back, covering the baby apple trees and mulching the new herb areas. The wrought-iron patio furniture should be dragged into the detached garage or would risk rusting completely in the sea-spray gales. By starting in the back, Ted knew, he lessened his chances of exposure.

The houses on either side of the driveway being empty, Mrs Oakapple was the only neighbor able to overlook Delilah's back garden, and Ted knew she was sympathetic to his cause. She'd had Ray Ramirez deliver a spice cake to Ted's house – not the station. One or two anonymous casseroles had appeared as well, but everyone knew Mrs Oakapple's nutmeg pound cake. It was as good as a signed confession.

Ted recognized, as he placed newspaper in the path between rows of what had been eggplants, that the cake was the only confession of sympathy he'd ever receive. Delilah's note on the mantel, addressed to no one, meant for everyone, would never be enough for Ted. But he knew Delilah, or he had, maybe. She thought thanks sufficient. She thought the pleasure of her company enough, never realizing that to Ted and possibly to Alan...

'That bastard,' Ted said as he stomped the damp paper into place. To Ted the pleasure of her company had felt like the promise of a future, not a payment for the present services rendered.

Delilah had written that she would miss him. Ted would have liked to believe that, but he thought most likely he'd never be able to, not really. Delilah finished her garden and moved on, Ted's theory went. He'd have to take comfort of a sort, a bitter sort, in the thought that he'd helped her. In the future, every time she thought of her island garden she'd also have to think of Ted. Would that be missing him? Ted supposed it depended on how much help Anton gave in her new garden. The marshal, in some strange burst of un-law-enforcement-officer-like pity, similar to the phone call telling Ted to call off the BOLO, had called back again. Delilah was safe, they both were safe, and neither was coming back. Ted didn't know why she'd told him. Maybe the marshal would call again and Ted could ask her. He'd like to talk to her again. She'd said she grew roses. Ted stomped the final piece of damp newspaper into the soil.

He was almost done in his own garden, and half the day was left to live through. He was going to go across the island and put Delilah's garden to rest. He'd do what he could for her, still. Maybe the 'I'll miss you' was a sop to his ego on her part, but missing her was quite real for him. Ted changed his mind: he would start in the front kitchen garden. Giving the villagers something to talk about over the icy winter would be just another service their sheriff could provide for them.

Ted wound up the garden hose and placed his shovel carefully on its hook in the shed. He didn't bother to go back inside his quiet house. There was nothing in there that he needed. He hopped into his official cruiser, not his truck, and started across the island to the empty cottage. He would park in the driveway for everyone to see.

The chain and the *PRIVATE PROPERTY* sign had disappeared with Delilah. It was the only part of the whole story that the islanders found strange, but then they'd never understood what happened on either side of that driveway. Ted could have told them, had they not been too discreet to ask, but his reticence and their stoicism prevented questions. Before long, the wind and the sand would obscure the gravel, and the driveway would once more be an open path to the beach. New residents might wonder about the cement posts guarding the entrance, but if they asked the islanders, they wouldn't be told the story.

The girl might only have been an islander a short while, but she deserved her privacy no less than the others. Her story was her own. And the islanders kept their stories to themselves.

Acknowledgements

Thank you to Laura Shanahan, Sarah Shaw, Daniela Ferrante, Beccy Fish, Louise Boland, Daniela Nava, and all the other geniuses at Fairlight Books. Delilah wouldn't exist without you.

Thank you to Tod Goldberg and Agam Patel for building what is essentially an ongoing support group for neurotic writers: the University of California, Riverside/Palm Desert Master of Fine Arts Program.

Thank you to those who talked me off many ledges of various heights, ofttimes on a daily basis, while I was writing this novel: Kit-Bacon Gressitt, Kelly Shire, Michael Scott Moore, Rebecca Klempner, Lorelei Laird and Maggie Downs. You only rolled your eyes at me a little.

Thank you to my fellow editors at Writers Resist for taking up my slack: Kit-Bacon Gressitt (she gets thanked twice because she's fabulous), Ying Wu, Debbie Hall and DW McKinney.

Thank you to Anjelica Ibarra and to Jason Metz for the slang and the regional vernacular.

Thank you to my husband, who still thinks there should be more sex scenes and more discussion of power tools – but not in that order.

Thank you to my mother, who is in no way similar to Abuela, not even a tiny wee bit, not at all, *nunca pero nunca*. Nohow.

And thank you to Gladys Uri, who died the day after she learned this book was coming. Thank you for waiting, dear friend. *Adelante*.

About the Author

Sara Marchant received her MFA in Creative Writing and Writing for the Performing Arts from the University of California, Riverside. She is the author of a memoir, *Proof of Loss* (2019), and a novella, *The Driveway Has Two Sides* (2018), on which *Becoming Delilah* is based. Her work has been published in journals including *The Coachella Review* and *Desert Magazine*, and in anthologies including *All the Women in My Family Sing* and the *Running Wild Novella Anthology*. She is a founding editor of the feminist literary collective and magazine *Writers Resist*.

JT TORRES
Taking Flight

When Tito is a child, his grandmother teaches him how to weave magic around the ones you love in order to keep them close. She is the master and he is the pupil, exasperating Tito's put-upon mother who is usually the focus of their mischief.

As Tito grows older and his grandmother's mind becomes less sound, their games take a dangerous turn. They both struggle with a particular spell, one that creates an illusion of illness to draw in love. But as the lines between magic and childish tales blur, so too do those between fantasy and reality.

'*Torres's masterful prose, and his inspired confrontation with grief and alienation, will linger in my mind for a long time*'
—Amy Kurtzweil, author of *Flying Couch: A Graphic Memoir*

'Taking Flight *stirs the heart with the revelation that when it comes to the greatest illusions in life, the real magic exists only because of love*'
—Don Reardon, author of *The Raven's Gift*

LORRAINE WILSON

Mother Sea

In an island community facing extinction, can hope rise stronger than grief?

Sisi de Mathilde lives on a remote island in the Indian Ocean. With the seas rising, the birth rate plummeting and her community under threat, she works as a scientist, reporting on local climate conditions to help protect her island home. But her life is thrown into turmoil when she finds herself newly widowed and unexpectedly pregnant.

When a group of outsiders arrive and try to persuade her community to abandon the island, Sisi is caught between the sacred 'old ways' of her ancestors and the possibilities offered by the outside world. As tensions rise and the islanders turn on one another, Sisi must fight to save her home, her people and her unborn child.

'Lyrical, moving, and at times haunting'
—Awais Khan, author of *No Honour*

'Complex, rich and beautifully crafted'
—Claire North, author of *The First Fifteen Lives of Harry August*